KAIJU RAMPAGE

ERIC S BROWN

SEVERED PRESS
HOBART TASMANIA

KAIJU RAMPAGE

WWW.SEVEREDPRESS.COM

ISBN: 978-1-925493-51-1

KAIJU RAMPAGE

Captain Daichi watched his crew hard at work on the deck of the *Hiroaka*. The day had just begun, but already the ship's hold was filling up with fish from her nets. Daichi had never seen the kind of loads his men were hauling now before in his life. It was almost as if something out there in the water was driving the fish his way. He whispered a prayer of thanks and smiled. This was Daichi's first run as captain. He had feared he would not live up to the expectations of his father and let the old man down. Even at the age of thirty-one, Daichi was somewhat afraid of the old man. Though his father was pushing eighty, he could still make his words cut deeper than the sharpest of swords.

The two of them had never seen eye to eye. Daichi had never wanted to be a part of his father's fishing company, much less the captain of the old man's best remaining boat. Daichi had dreamed of being a writer, going to America, and becoming a star. At first, he had some success. He had sold his first ever story to a paying magazine and almost immediately got an offer to write one for another. That sort of thing was rare in the writing world, and Daichi allowed himself to believe that he could make it. He spent the next few years doing his best. His work sold, he made money, but it was never quite enough or dependable enough to be all he did in terms of a job.

Daichi's father had been there for him, if at a price. His father had given him just enough work to keep him afloat and chasing his dream for a time. After five years had passed, his father became more and more demanding of him, pushing more and more work onto him. His father's health had begun to fail with age. The old man needed someone who could take over and continue to bring honor to the family name. Daichi was the only son. He had three sisters, but his father wanted him, not them. His father held with the old ways and wanted Daichi to surrender his failed dream to step up and do what he had been born to do.

When this fishing season had started, the old man had given Daichi a choice. Take over as captain of the *Hiroaka* or leave the family business behind for good. Daichi had known it was no idle threat. Either he stepped up or he was out. His self-published sales were down, and short stories weren't paying what they used to, not that it had ever been enough. With his rent already close to being late and a stack of bills on his desk, Daichi was left with no choice. Now, here he was on the deck of the *Hiroaka*, doing the job he had sworn as a child he would never do.

The *Hiroaka* was an old ship, only weighing in at a displacement of around one hundred and fifty tons. Her entire crew, counting Daichi himself, was composed of two dozen sailors. She ran nearly one hundred feet from bow to stern. What she lacked in size and crew, though, she more than made up for in the tech aboard her. Her sonar and comm. gear was top of the line. That fact was one of the few things Daichi liked about her.

Natsuo approached him wearing a concerned expression that gave Daichi cause for worry.

"Good morning, Natsuo," Daichi offered.

"Captain Daichi, sir," Natsuo responded with a quick nod of his head. "I would be most grateful if you would accompany me inside."

"Is my father calling again?" Daichi asked. His old man, though wheelchair bound, had followed him to sea in a sense, thanks to the very state of the art gear that Daichi liked that the *Hiroaka* had onboard. Even in the worst of storms, the ship's communications worked flawlessly.

"No, Captain Daichi," Natsuo told him. "There is something you must see."

Daichi grunted his consent and moved to follow Natsuo to the heart of the small ship where her helm controls and sonar station were. Tomo, the ship's comm. and sonar specialist, was there waiting for them. Tomo got up from his station as Daichi entered. He gave Daichi a quick bow of respect.

"What is it, Tomo?" Daichi asked. "Natsuo has been rather vague about why you needed me here."

"With good cause, Captain," Tomo said. "We did not want to cause a panic."

Daichi's eyebrows rose at the bizarre disclosure. "Panic? What are you talking about, Tomo?"

"Look for yourself, sir," Tomo told him, gesturing at the sonar screen.

Daichi studied the screen. At first, he didn't have a clue what Tomo was trying to show him, but then he saw it. The blip was so large Daichi had thought it was just part of the screen.

"What is that?" he asked.

"We don't know, Captain," Natsuo told him. "Whatever it is, though, it's coming straight for us."

"And fast, too," Tomo added. "It's moving at twenty knots."

Daichi glanced back at the sonar screen, quickly doing the math in his head. "So we have about ten minutes until whatever that is reaches us?"

Tomo and Natsuo nodded in unison.

"Could it be a ship?" Daichi asked. "Have you tried hailing it?"

"I don't think it's a ship, sir," Tomo said. "Something about the way it moves. . ."

"We have tried making contact with it, Captain," Natsuo informed him. "On every channel available to us. There has been no reply."

Daichi rubbed at his cheeks with the fingers and thumb of his right hand. "I am man enough to admit I don't have an answer to this one. Both of you are more experienced with all this. What do you suggest we do?"

"Run, Captain," Tomo said almost instantly. "We certainly can't fight something that size and that fast if it's hostile. The *Hiroaka* is a fishing boat. Yes, we have some small arms aboard in case of pirates but nothing that could give us a chance against something like that."

"I have to agree, sir," Natsuo nodded.

"The men are in the middle of pulling up the nets," Daichi protested. "All the fish in them here will be lost if we run. And what we will tell the rest of the crew? Won't running cause exactly the sort of panic you were hoping to avoid?"

Neither Natsuo nor Tomo had an answer.

"You said this thing is moving at twenty knots correct?" Daichi asked, still weighing his course of action.

"Yes, Captain," Tomo replied.

"The *Hiroaka*'s max speed with her engines at full is only eighteen knots," Daichi reminded them. "If we run and whatever that thing is decides to come after us, we won't be able to outrun it."

Natsuo and Tomo stared at him, waiting for his orders.

"The call is yours, sir," Natsuo said. "Whatever you decide to do, though, Captain, I suggest we do it quickly."

"Fine," Daichi grunted. "Tell the crew what's going on and pass out what weapons we do have aboard. There's no point in keeping them in the dark at this point. They'll know something is badly wrong as soon as we give the order to abandon the nets."

Daichi paused, taking a breath before continuing. It hurt him to give up the fish, but he could see no other option. "Tell them to drop the nets. Tomo, get down to the engines and make sure we get all the speed out of them that we can. Natsuo, set a course away from whatever that thing, maximum speed."

Tomo and Natsuo hurried to carry out his orders while Daichi moved to watch the chaos that began on the ship's deck as soon as Natsuo started barking orders through the loudspeakers.

The crew outside looked absolutely terrified as they cut loose the nets they had been reeling up. He could see in their faces, even from where he was looking out the window of the small control room of the ship. The fear in those expressions only grew as Natsuo ordered the men to pass out the weapons from the ship's weapon lockers.

Daichi's attention became focused on the horizon beyond the *Hiroaka*'s forward deck. He picked up a nearby pair of binoculars and raised them to his eyes. Out there in the distance, he could see the something massive cutting through the waves towards the ship. Daichi felt sick as the full scale of its size sunk in. The thing was many, many times the size of the *Hiroaka*.

Natsuo was spinning the wheel around madly, turning the *Hiroaka* away from the approaching contact. Daichi could already see that even with the engines straining at full power, it wasn't going to be enough.

Some of the sailors on the deck who had already been given small arms opened fire at the massive creature streaking towards the ship. Shotguns thundered and pistols cracked rapid succession. Daichi had to bite his lip to keep from laughing at how futile their shots seemed given the size of the thing coming at them.

In the last instant before the creature plowed into the *Hiroaka*, it rose partially up out of the waves. Its head was horned. A great horn protruded from each side of its skull, and a third larger one rose from the middle of its forehead. Its body was covered in thick scales that reminded Daichi of the scales of python, all yellow and black. It gave a roar that left everyone aboard the *Hiroaka* screaming in pain and clutching their ears before the creature dropped its head back into the water. The window in front of Daichi blew out. Shards of glass exploded, burying them in his flesh. Blood spurted in splashes of bright red from one piece ripped open the side of his neck. Daichi stumbled backwards to collapse onto the floor.

The monster struck the *Hiroaka* at a speed well over twenty knots. The hull of the fishing vessel folded inward with the squeals of rending metal. The impact was so great that the *Hiroaka* was lifted from the surface of the ocean and sent toppling over onto its side before it completely broke apart as the monster plowed through it, tearing it to pieces.

****

General Akio watched the floor indicator of the elevator slowly clicking upwards. He felt as if he were slicked with sweat despite the cool of the air conditioning that kept the building at a comfortable sixty-eight degrees, no matter how hot the summer day grew outside. The fingers of his right hand clutched the handle of the armored briefcase he carried. Akio was not looking forward to his meeting with Director Daisuke. Daisuke was one of the most powerful men in Tokyo. He owned this entire building, and the full wealth and power of the Rao Corporation was his to command. The job had fallen to Akio to be the one to deliver the news to him that monsters were real, and they were on their way to this very city. Akio could only pray that Diasuke wasn't the sort who took out the anger wrought by the message upon the messenger. It was not as if Akio had no power of his own. He was a general. Still, there were other means that men such as Daisuke could extract their vengeance if they felt they needed to do so to keep their honor intact.

The elevator doors opened onto the top floor of the Rao building. Akio steeled himself and plunged through them into the vast waiting area beyond. At the far end of the room, a lone secretary sat at an antique and luxurious desk. Her long black hair was pulled tightly atop her head into a bun. She wore thick, though stylish, glasses. She looked up from her work to greet him with a smile as Akio marched towards her. The two of them were not alone. Two well-dressed and clearly armed security personnel stood not far behind her desk, guarding the entrance to Daisuke's office.

"Good afternoon, General Akio," the sectary purred. "Mr. Daisuke is expecting you. You may enter whenever you are ready."

The two guards stopped him as he started for the door.

"I'm sorry, sir," one of them said, but Akio knew the man wasn't sorry. If anything, the gun for hire merc was having the time of his life getting to frisk a full-fledged general. Akio endured the weapons search with nothing more than a frown, though inwardly he imagined putting the two guards into their place. He was young for a general and had risen to his position by killing enemies of the state, not pushing papers with his butt in a chair. Akio seriously believed he could take them both at once.

"He's clean," the smaller of the two guards said.

The other nodded and gestured towards the office doors. "You may go on in now, sir."

The doors opened on their own as General Akio walked to them and on through them into Daisuke's office. The office was the epitome of the word grandiose. Large tanks of exotic fish lined its walls and scores of American comic books, framed and sealed in protective casings, hung above them. The lighting of the room was dim and twelve foot tall, twenty-four feet wide window behind Daisuke's desk shaded to block the rays of the sun.

Director Daisuke sat behind his desk watching him closely as Akio strolled across the long distance towards his desk to ultimately take a seat in the empty chair in front of it.

"Greetings, General." Daisuke grinned, flashing too-white teeth.

"Director," Akio acknowledged him. "I wish I was here under better circumstances."

"Exactly what are the circumstances that bring you here, General?" Daisuke asked.

"May I?" Akio asked, lifting his briefcase for Daisuke's approval.

"But of course," Daisuke assured him.

Akio sat the briefcase on Daisuke desk and keyed in the three series of codes needed to open it. With the completion of each sequence, there was the audible snap of a lock opening. When he was done, Akio spun the briefcase around so that Daisuke could see the visual screen that lined its top.

"What I am about to show you, Director Daisuke, is classified and—"

"I am aware of the protocols, General. Do get on with it," Daisuke ordered him.

"These images were taken yesterday morning," Akio said as he activated the screen inside the briefcase. It came to life showing a grizzly scene of bodies floating, being bounced about on the waves. The images were rough and shaky as if being shot from a handheld device, close up. The image zoomed out to show a large body of debris that appeared to have once been a ship then altered again to show everything from a viewpoint high above the wreckage to give it scale. From this angle, the rescue boats that were clearly shooting the original set of images could be seen.

"What am I looking at here, General Aiko?" Daisuke asked, "And more importantly, why?"

General Akio chose his words carefully. "Director Daisuke, the government has known of your Project Kaiju for some time. The fishing vessel in those images was completely destroyed with all hands aboard just off the coast yesterday morning. All signs point to something massive, moving at high speed, ramming into it."

Daisuke leaned back in his chair with a smirk on his lips. "Are you accusing the Daisuke Corporation of being involved in the deaths of these sailors, General?"

"No, Director, at least not at this time," Aiko answered honestly. "However, surely you can see why my superiors would want you questioned about this incident."

"Project Kaiju was discontinued when my father passed on, General," Daisuke said. "We here at the Daisuke Corporation no longer waste resources on the sort of genetic engineering that project involved."

General Akio cleared his throat. "As you say, Director, but the Daisuke Corporation remains under contract as an advanced weapons designer for all branches of Japan's military."

"I understand your concern, General Akio, I do." Daisuke frowned. "But this corporation, as I said, has taken a different path under my direction."

"Director Daisuke, the attack on this fishing vessel is not an isolated incident. There have been two more inside of the last forty-eight hours and close to two dozen in the last week. Each such attack has been closer to our nation than the last. All of these attacks seem to be caused by *something* massive and intelligent that appears to be on direct course for our nation and this very city."

Daisuke tilted his head, as if appraising him more intently. "And you believe this city may be in danger?"

"All evidence points to that, Director Daisuke." Akio met the director's eyes. "We were hoping that your corporation might have some knowledge about whatever is behind these attacks so we can be better prepared to stand against whatever it is once it reaches Tokyo."

"There is an American carrier group just south of this island, General. May I suggest that your time would be better spent rallying them to our aid than here chasing shadows?"

"I will be approaching the Americans as soon as I am through here, Director. You can count on that," Akio said firmly.

"See that you do," Daisuke ordered, though he possessed no real power to do so. "Now if you will let yourself out, General, I have work which I need to attend to. Good day."

"Good day, Director." Akio kept himself polite as he rose from his seat and left Daisuke's office.

****

Admiral Travis Hall sat in the command chair about the USS *Lee*. The *Lee* was the heart and center of the carrier strike group known as Task force Gamma Red. She carried seventy aircraft aboard her, a mix of fighters and helicopters. The rest of the task force was composed of four destroyers: the USS *Harden*, the USS *Wellington*, the USS *Curtis,* and the USS *Kirby*. The four destroyers were spread out in a defensive formation around the *Lee*. The United States and Japan were allies, but Admiral Hall was the type of commanding officer who liked to be prepared at all times. His habit of doing so had saved his life and those of his crews more than once in his career. The last twenty-four hours had been anything but usual. His communication officers over the last two shifts had picked up the desperate and dying cries of the crews of several civilian boats not too far away. Each attack had appeared completely unprovoked, catching the stricken vessels utterly by surprise. And each attack had been just as deadly. As far as Admiral Hall knew based on the reports, it didn't sound like a single ship had survived once attacked. He had dispatched two Seahawks to recon the location of the closest attack to the task force's position, but they had been intercepted by Japanese fighters and ordered to return to the *Lee*. Whatever was happening out there, the Japanese were playing their cards close to their chest about it.

Just before noon, a Japanese destroyer group, consisting of four Atago-class vessels, was detected approaching the task force. The DESRON closed to within a few miles and was now operating on a parallel course to it. The DESRON had identified itself as Samurai II and assured Admiral Hall that its intent was not hostile. Commander Hiroto, when questioned, would give no reasonable explanation for the actions of the DESRON under his command. When Admiral Hall had inquired about the transmissions his task force had intercepted and offered assistance, Commander Hiroto not only refused help, but wouldn't comment on the obvious attacks occurring in Japanese waters beyond to politely suggest that they were not of concern to Task force Gamma Red.

Two Kawasaki OH-1 Ninjas accompanying a Chinook had appeared on the *Lee*'s radar not long after Commander Hiroto's DESRON had settled in running alongside Task force Gamma Red.

"Admiral," Hall's XO, Dodson, approached him. "We have an incoming transmission from the Chinook that just showed up on our screens. It's requesting permission to land aboard the *Lee*."

Hall gave his XO a questioning look.

"It claims to have General Akio of the Japanese Defense Force aboard it."

"Permission granted," Hall told Dodson. "Perhaps this General Akio will be willing to tell us what in the devil is going on out here."

"I wouldn't count on it, sir." Dodson smiled.

"Allow me my hopes." Hall shot his XO a smile. "Bring the general to my ready room as soon as he's aboard."

****

General Akio was much younger than Admiral Hall had imagined he would be. Akio moved with a cat-like grace as he entered Hall's ready room. Hall watched him glance around, taking in his surrounding with a keen eye.

Admiral Hall rose and gave him a polite bow. "Welcome aboard, General."

Hall gestured at the seat in front of his desk. General Akio accepted the offer as Hall returned to his own seat.

"To what do I owe this honor, General?"

"There is a situation growing in these waters, Admiral. One that I fear will soon spiral beyond our control," Akio told him bluntly.

"I gathered as much," Hall commented. "We've been monitoring civilian radio traffic in the area."

"Then you already know of the attacks?" General Akio asked.

Hall nodded. "Yes, we do, though we are clueless to why they are happening or who is behind them. I have extended an offer of aid to the commander of your DESRON." Hall titled his head westward to where the mentioned DESRON was running along beside his task force. "It was refused without reason."

"Commander Hiroto was only acting out of a sense of caution, Admiral. In his place, you would have surely done the same. His orders forbid him from accepting American aid until I arrived to, um, discuss the current situation occurring in these waters with you directly."

"I understand that, General, and I sympathize; however, if this situation you speak of is a possible threat to the ships under my command, I expect to be fully informed of its nature now that you *are* here." Hall made sure his tone was professional despite the growing frustration he was feeling.

"The truth, Admiral," Akio frowned, "the truth is that we aren't entirely surely what is happening out here ourselves, though we do have our suspicions as to what is behind the attacks on our ships."

Hall stared at the general waiting on him to continue.

"Admiral Hall, have you ever heard the word Kaiju before?" General Akio asked.

Hall couldn't stop himself. He burst into laughter before he even realized he had. It took a great deal of effort to stop. When he did, he composed himself hurriedly.

"Forgive me, General," Hall apologized.

"I see you have heard the word before, Admiral," Akio said coldly.

"Yes, General, I have," Hall admitted. "I believe it refers to a kind of strange, giant monster."

"You would be correct in that assumption," Akio confirmed.

"Surely you aren't suggesting that a real Kaiju is the cause of these attacks?"

When the general didn't answer straight away, Hall blinked in surprise. Akio's expression was that of a man who believed he knew the truth and was being mocked for it.

"And if I was?" Akio said at last.

Admiral Hall thought over his answer before he spoke it. "I would want proof."

Akio nodded slowly and then gave a soft chuckle of his own. "I am afraid any proof I could offer you, Admiral Hall, is classified too highly to be shared with even an ally such as yourself. I can, however, assure that Kaiju are very real, as real as you and I. Japan has dealt with them before and will likely continue to do so until a means can be found to eliminate the entirety of their kind from the Earth."

Though he could see Akio was serious, and his every instinct assured him of that fact, Admiral Hall still wondered if the general was playing some sort of game with him.

"General, if I understand you correctly, you're actually saying these attacks are the result of an active, real life Kaiju in Japanese waters," Admiral Hall said.

"Yes, Admiral, that is exactly what I am saying, except that I never said it was merely one Kaiju." Akio frowned. "I believe we are dealing with much more than a single monster."

Admiral Hall rocked himself back in his chair, his mind reeling from Akio's admission.

"Now that you know what we are up against, if your offer of assistance still stands, Admiral, I would like to accept it officially on behalf of the government of my nation," Akio said with a straight face.

Hall didn't know what to say to so he stalled for time. "I'll have to check with my superiors, General Akio. I'll be in touch when I have done so. At this point, I can't commit to anything more."

Akio gave him a sharp nod and rose from his chair. "I understand, Admiral. Just keep in mind that time is likely something we don't have much of. The hour is late, and the

Kaiju may come for you, unless you leave these waters, just as they have in my nation."

Pausing at the door of Hall's ready room before he exited, General Akio turned back to say, "Keep your crews alert, Admiral. If you've been monitoring the attacks as you claim, then you know just how and unexpectedly the Kaiju strike."

And with that, the general was gone, leaving Admiral Hall sitting alone and stunned behind his desk.

****

General Akio's security escort rejoined him as he walked across the main flight deck of the USS *Lee* to climb inside the Chinook he had come aboard on. He took his seat, strapping himself in, as the pilot fired up the copter. It rose smoothly from the carrier's deck, heading back towards Tokyo. The two Ninjas swung into a protective formation around it. Akio had taken a seat that gave him a clear view of the ocean, and he sat staring out at the waves, lost in his thoughts. He had done all he could to enlist the aid of the American carrier group. Asking the Americans for help wasn't the ideal thing to do, but he would take whatever aid he could get. The largest kaiju attack of the past century had wiped out wiped out Task Group 81.12 a decade ago. The military working with the government and press had managed to keep the incident from the public and the world at large, but the attack had still cost Japan four submarines with no confirmed Kaiju kill to show for it. His gut told him this was going to get much, much worse when the kaiju opted to truly show themselves.

The data on the current attacks on civilian vessels thus far pointed to there being far more than one kaiju in play. Akio wasn't a scientist or crypto-biologist, but he knew the lore of the kaiju. His grandfather had told him stories about the giant monsters throughout his youth long before Akio reached his current rank to discover that such monsters were indeed much more than mere folklore. It chilled him to his core that his homeland was quite possibly facing a full out attack by a *group* of such monsters. If one kaiju could take out four submarines and survive, what could a group of them do if they made landfall on Japan? Akio did not want to find out. As thus, his plan was to engage and stop them long before they reached Japan's coast, and with the current disposition of Japanese forces, he was forced to admit that he needed the Americans' help.

Another question that tore at his mind was what kind of kaiju he was dealing with. He knew from both the classified reports he had been given access to as well as folklore that no two kaiju tended to be alike. Each creature was usually unique with different powers, for lack of a better word, and tendencies. There was just no way of knowing what was heading for Tokyo until either he was able to directly engage the kaiju head on or the monsters opted to expose themselves of their own accord.

The powers that be had given him carte blanche in terms of assembling Tokyo's defense. He had placed all the fighter craft in the area on alert and, in addition to sending Commander Hiroto's DESRON to join up with the American Task force, had positioned DESRONs 83 and 89 in the path of the approaching Kaiju just off the coast. In his heart, General Akio didn't believe it would be enough, but with so little time, it was the best he could manage.

He hadn't written off the Daisuke Corporation yet, though. Director Daisuke might claim that Project Kaiju had been discontinued when he had taken over for his father a few years back, but Akio didn't believe him. He couldn't press the issue as of yet, but if the kaiju made it through the defenses he was arranging, it would be interesting to see how Director Daisuke reacted to the kaiju showing up in his city. His corporation had too great of a vested interest in Tokyo to allow the city to burn. Whatever Daisuke was hiding, Akio would almost bet his life that Daisuke would use whatever he had at his disposal.

"General!" the Chinook's pilot called to him. "We've got incoming!"

It took Akio a moment to process the words. He looked up from his thoughts and saw the *thing* approaching the trio of helicopters that the Chinook he was aboard was in the center of. Akio had never seen anything like it in his life. It appeared to be part bird and part lizard. The creature's wingspan was easily 50 feet across. Akio's heart nearly froze in his chest as he saw the creature wasn't alone.

The Chinook broke hard out of the formation as the two Ninjas veered to engage the inbound monsters. Their forward cannons opened up, bright tracer rounds streaking through the air. The barrage of high-velocity rounds ripped towards the monsters, but they were too fast. They rolled in the air, dodging the hailstorm of lead.

The monsters came in fast, shrieking cries that sounded like high-pitched whistles. One of them plowed directly into the closer of the two Ninjas. The copter and the monster vanished in a blossoming ball of flame and flying debris.

"Gods help us!" Akio heard his pilot cry as the man continued to try to pour on speed and get the Chinook out of the combat zone.

Akio twisted in his seat to try to look back at the remaining Ninja as missiles flew from its wings towards one of the monsters. The bird-like beast tried to dodge again, but this time was too slow. The missiles struck it dead on. The creature exploded in a mass of charred bone and tissue that spun away from the center of the blast.

"Get me a line to the Americans!" Akio shouted. "They're the only ones closer enough to help."

****

Admiral Hall emerged from his ready room, scowling. His XO, Dodson, was waiting for him.

"I take it things did not go well, sir." Dodson grinned.

"I just told the powers that be back home that the Japanese military sent a general aboard this ship to ask for our assistance in fighting giant monsters. To say it didn't go well might be the understatement of the eon."

Admiral Hall eased into his command chair.

"Well, the suspense is killing me, sir?" Dodson urged. "What are our orders?"

"Believe it or not," Hall said, "they want us to render any assistance we can. I don't think they believe General Akio's story any more than we do, but the Japanese are our allies."

Dodson shrugged. "Could be worse I suppose."

Hall frowned. "Maybe."

"Sir, incoming transmission from General Akio!" Hall's Comm. Officer, Williamson, shouted.

It didn't take a genius to see that the call was urgent.

"Put it through," Hall ordered.

"This is General Akio aboard the Behemoth," Akio voice was panicked. "We are under attack and are in need of emergency assistance."

"I've got the Japanese birds on radar, Admiral," Dixon informed him before Hall could ask.

"The three copters appear to be engaged with a large, unidentified contact," Dixon continued.

"Launch all Ready Five fighters," Hall ordered. "I want them in the air now."

"Yes, sir," Dodson replied and moved to get the fighters rolling.

Three Super Hornets screamed their way into flight leaving the deck of USS *Lee.* Admiral Hall watched them go.

Admiral Hall left his command chair and moved to stand beside Williamson at the radar station.

"This is Jackal. ETA in two," Captain Clarkson's voice came over the comm.

Hall's eyes were focused on the radar screen. "What the Hell is the contact?"

Williamson had real no answer. "I don't know, sir, but it's big, and it's fast."

Admiral Hall and Williamson listened in on the comm. chatter of the Jackal squadron as the Super Hornets neared the scene of the battle.

"Did you see that?" Jackal Two cried.

"Sweet mother!" Jackal Three chimed in. "What in the devil are those things?"

"Focus!" Jackal One snapped. "Prepare to engage!"

"One of them just overtook that Ninja like it was standing still and knocked it out of the sky!" Jackal Three reported.

"I got tone!" Jackal Two said. "Firing!"

"Watch the Chinook! Watch the Chinook!" Jackal One was yelling.

"Somebody tell that idiot to get out of there!" Jackal Two spat.

"The big one is on my tail!" Jackal Three screamed. "Get it off! Get it off!"

There was the sound of crunching metal over the comm. followed by a scream that was cut suddenly short. Jackal Three vanished from the radar screen in a flash.

"That thing got Jake!" Jackal Two shouted.

"Focus! Blast it!" Jackal One ordered.

Admiral Hall watched another of the unknown contacts disappear from the radar screen. That only left two more. *At least the odds were even now,* he thought.

"Coming around!" Jackal One called.

"Watch it! Watch it!" Jackal Two was screaming.

Jackal One and another unknown contact vanished together.

Another minute later, the battle was over.

"This is Jackal Two to the *Lee*," the pilot, Bridger, transmitted.

"This is the *Lee*," Admiral Hall responded. "Report Status."

"Jackals One and Three have been lost as well as the two birds that were flying escort for the Chinook. The enemy has been eliminated, though, sir. Should I accompany the general's bird on to Tokyo?"

"No," Admiral Hall ordered. "You've done your job. Get back here at full burn."

"Yes, sir," Bridger answered. "Jackal Two, heading home."

****

Admiral Hall had Bridger report his ready room as soon as the pilot was back aboard. Hall left Dodson in command of the *Lee* with the ship on full alert as he met Bridger there. The pilot was clearly rattled. Sweat slicked his skin and matted his dark, black hair to his head.

"You wanted to see me, Admiral?" Bridger asked.

"Have a seat, son," Hall told him, handing him a glass of iced water.

Bridger chugged at it madly, consuming two-thirds of it before sitting it on the edge of Hall's desk.

"Thank you, sir," the pilot said.

"What the heck happened out there?" Hall asked. "No BS. Just the facts."

"Yes, sir," Bridger nodded. "We were inbound towards the position of the Japanese forces. That's when we saw them."

Bridger's expression was a mixture of fear, disgust, and disbelief as he spoke. "They were like giant birds, sir. Er, well, more like giant flying lizards."

"Have your flight crew send me the video from your flight," Hall ordered and then took a second to study Bridger closer before continuing. "So, you're saying Jackal One and Jackal Two were taken out by monsters."

"Yes, sir, I am," Bridger answered firmly. "Whatever those things were well... They shouldn't be real, sir, but they are."

"How did they take out the other members of your squadron lieutenant?"

"The Ninja we saw destroyed on our approach and Jackal One were both taken out by the bird things slamming into them. The monsters didn't seem to care or understand they would die in the process."

"And Jackal Two?"

Bridger shook his head. "One of those things flew up on Jackal Two from its rear. It overtook Jordon's Hornet and came in above it, matching its speed..."

Hall could see that Bridger was utterly terrified of the memory of what he had seen.

"And then?" Hall pressed, unable to afford the pilot any compassion due to the danger of the situation they were all in now. It appeared the kaiju General Akio had told him about were apparently truly real.

"That thing grabbed ahold of Jordon's plane from above it. The huge talons of its feet sunk into and through the metal of the Hornet . . ." Bridger looked him in the eye. "It just ripped the Hornet apart, sir."

"I see," Hall said, feeling far more sympathy for the pilot than he was allowing himself to show. "You're dismissed, Bridger. Go get some rest and clear your head."

"Yes, sir. Thank you, sir," Bridger said and hurried from the room.

Hall watched the pilot go. It was hard to believe that kaiju were real, but there was unquestionable evidence of the fact now. The *Lee* and all the other ships of Task force Gamma Red were running on high alert, but Hall was at a loss as to what else to do. There were no set protocols for dealing with monsters, and though he could radio those above him, in the end, he was the CO on the scene, and the hard calls were going to be his.

His hand reached for the drawer of his desk where he kept a bottle of Vodka tucked away but stopped. A hit might take the edge off the stress he was under, but he needed to stay sharp, sharper than ever. He was used to fighting other men, not mythological creatures. Only God knew where the things might strike next or how they would do it when they did.

Hall needed to talk with General Akio as soon as possible. The general was in route to Tokyo. The Chinook he was aboard was high-tailing it there at top speed. With General Akio unavailable, Hall supposed the CO of the Japanese DESRON shadowing his task force would have to do.

****

Commander Hiroto was shocked by the American admiral's request to come aboard his flagship of the Samurai II DESRON. He couldn't refuse, however. General Akio had made it very clear that Hiroto was to do everything in his power to help bring the Americans into the coming fight against the kaiju. He met Admiral Hall personally and escorted him to a sealed briefing room where they could discuss the matters at hand securely.

"I understand that you sent some of your planes to aid General Akio," Commander Hiroto commented as the two men seats across from each other at the room's sole table.

"Three F-18 Super Hornets left the flight deck of the *Lee*, Commander," Hall said. "Only one made it home."

"I am very sorry for your losses, Admiral, but grateful for your help. Losing General Akio, now, would be a very bad thing for all of Tokyo and perhaps all of Japan as well."

"I'll be honest and admit that I didn't believe the general when he came aboard my ship sprouting nonsense about giant monsters," Admiral Hall said, frowning.

"But now you know they are real," Commander Hiroto finished for him.

"Something is out there, that's for sure," Hall replied. "My pilot, Bridger—he was the only one to make it back to the *Lee* in the wake of the engagement with the things that attacked your general's fleet of helicopters. He certainly believes that kaiju are real. I had the video flight unit pulled from his F-18," Hall shrugged, "and I can't explain the creatures I saw on it. Nothing like those things should exist in the real world."

"That is part of the danger of the kaiju, Admiral Hall," Commander Hiroto told him. "It was not easy for me to accept their existence either at first, and I had access to records of other attacks throughout Japan's history. Nonetheless, regardless of what we believe, the kaiju are coming. That is simply a fact. Can we count on your aid in stopping them before they reach Japan?"

"I've contacted my superiors and informed them of the situation here. My orders are to lend whatever assistance you need," Admiral Hall answered reluctantly.

"I see," Commander Hiroto said. "And you are unhappy with those orders?"

"I didn't say that, Commander," Admiral Hall growled. "America and Japan are allies. Task force Gamma Red will honor the obligations that come with that as long as it's under my command."

"Then I do not understand the hesitation I sense from you." Commander Hiroto rose an eyebrow at him.

"I don't like going into any kind of battle blind, Commander Hiroto. I am sure you can understand that," Hall explained. "I've fought a good deal of battles of in my day but never one against literal monsters before."

"I can indeed understand that, Admiral, but what would you have me do?" Commander Hiroto leaned forward in his seat.

"I am going to be endangering the lives under my command for the sake of your people, Commander Hiroto, therefore I would like to know all you about what it is we are up against."

"We don't know anything more about the kaiju headed for Japan at this moment than you do, Admiral. Every kaiju is different. No two are alike. Thus far, we've had no true engagement with them."

"Cut the crap, Hiroto," Hall snarled. "By your own admission, your people have fought the kaiju many times since the birth of your nation. I need to know what we are up against, blast it!"

Hiroto spread his hands in a gesture of peace. "Some kaiju are like those you see in the movies that both our people create. They are giant, lizard-like creatures that shake the earth itself with their steps. Others have wings, like the sort you have already fought. Still, others live solely in the water like your Krakens of myth. All of them are deadly. All of them are massive in scale compared to whatever animal or animals they share the characteristics of. And there are even kaiju who defy all logical explanation. One of your American writers wrote of these in his fiction. He told tales of gelatinous abominations that oozed over the land, consuming all in their path."

"Surely you must have some more specific idea of what we are up against than just a vague list of things that might be out there," Hall protested.

"I wish I did, Admiral. It would make all our jobs much easier, but as I have said, and it is the truth, we will not have a true understanding of the present kaiju behind these attacks until either we go have them or they show themselves as they come after our blood," Commander Hiroto explained. "We have no set protocols for an attack of this scale. That is why General Akio has been given the level of power that has been bestowed upon him. Even as he works to build a defense against the monsters approaching us, he is also at work determining just what they are and what has drawn them from their slumber towards Japan in such great numbers after so long a time without an incident of this scale."

"See?" Admiral Hall argued. "You so much as admitted that you know this coming attack will be the worst in recent history for your people. How can you know that if you know nothing about the approaching kaiju?"

Commander Hiroto shrugged. "All evidence points to this being the largest attack ever on record. In the past, kaiju attacks have been limited to a single ship, fleet, or location. The monsters appear, ravage whatever they stumble upon, and vanish. This time, there seems a coordinated move towards Japan. Many locations and many ships have been attacked all along a route that leads to Tokyo."

"I've placed the ships of my task force on alert, Commander," Admiral Hall said. "And as I have said," he continued, trying to keep the frustration he was feeling out of his voice, "we are at your disposal, Commander Hiroto."

"Then we must set course for the coast at once. The ships of our combined forces will be Tokyo's primary defense. We will position ourselves to intercept the kaiju before they make landfall and wait for them there."

Admiral Hall snorted. "I suppose that is as a good a plan as any."

"It is all we can do," Commander Hiroto replied.

****

Three hours had passed since General Akio's helicopter fleet had been attacked. His Chinook had made it safely to Tokyo shortly thereafter. Akio's aide, Heather Karza, had already begun carrying out his orders for the defense of the city by the time he arrived. She was American by birth, though now a Japanese citizen and the most valuable member of his staff. Technically, she wasn't military but rather served as his advisor. The carte blanche level of power that Akio held in regards to the city of Tokyo, however, allowed her to act in his stead when his presence was required elsewhere, as it had been in his attempt to gain enlist the assistance of the American task force.

The forces General Akio had requisitioned were beginning to arrive, and it was impossible to conceal their presence. The cover story was simply "military maneuvers" being conducted in the city, but Akio knew that most of the populace of Tokyo wasn't stupid enough to fall for such a cover. If it was the United States, perhaps such a story would have worked, but not in Japan. He took pride in his nation, even as he cursed the fact that he needed a cover at all. The simplest course of action would have been to evacuate Tokyo and its surrounding areas, but with so much still unknown about the events that would be unfolding soon, his superiors didn't want to cause a panic. If the kaiju could be stopped offshore, then there was no need for such a massive undertaking and the risks that accompanied it.

His superiors continued to hope that the approaching kaiju could be met at sea and stopped there long before the creatures ever touched Japanese soil. Commander Hiroto had been in contact with him to inform him that the Americans had joined up, but even so, General Akio held his doubts that the kaiju could be stopped before they made landfall.

General Akio's Chinook had delivered him to the building he was using as his base of operations in the city. It was close enough to the coast for his temporary office to have an excellent view of the ocean. He stood at the office's window, staring out at the distant water.

"It's a mess out there, sir," he heard Karza say from behind him and turned to face her. As always, she was dressed in black to match the long black hair that slipped from her head to over her shoulders. Akio took a breath as he saw her. Karza was the kind of beauty that the poets of old wrote about. There was something almost angelic about her features. She was thin but toned and well proportioned. Karza looked to be around twenty-two, but Akio had never asked what her real age was. To do so would have been impolite and disrespectful, though he wagered she was far older than she appeared.

At first glance, one might take her as frail and a somewhat geeky type of girl. One look into those cold, hardened eyes of her, though, and that notion died quickly. Akio had worked with her long enough now to know that she was not to be angered. She might look like an angel, but if the woman had a soul, it was certainly far more demonic in nature than angelic.

"I am sure you have things well in hand." Akio gave her a slight bow.

"I didn't say anything to the contrary, sir," Karza told him bluntly. "I merely wanted to you to know that I fear things will be hitting a boiling point soon. The fifth, eighth, and tenth columns are in route to take up their arranged positions along the docks. The sixth, seventh, and ninth have already arrived at the beach. That many tanks rolling through a city like this one, though, sir, it's like setting off flares and screaming for the populace to panic."

"But so far things have remained calm," Akio pointed out.

"So far." Karza's voice was like ice. "We can't count on that continuing. I again suggest we declare martial law at once while it is still relatively easy to do so. When the panic does begin, armed troops in the streets may do more to stir the coming panic than calm it."

"I understand what you are saying, Heather," Akio said, calling her by her first name. "The powers that be aren't ready to resort to such a measure yet without better cause."

Karza gave him a look that told him exactly what she thought of the powers that be.

"Be that as it may, sir, you are in command here, not them."

"It'll be declared soon enough," he assured her. "Thank you for the update on the armored divisions. Are our other forces ready?"

"I have every available fighter and attack helicopter I could draft into our forces here on ready alert. The local authorities have been given their instructions, though they remain ignorant of the full scope of what is coming towards Tokyo. Commander Hiroto's Samurai II DESRON and the American task force should be in position as well within the hour."

"Then we've done all we can," General Akio sighed.

"Not everything, sir," Karza purred.

"Drop it, Heather," General Akio warned her. "You know that Daisuke is off limits, even to us."

"To you, sir," Karza grinned. "I'm not military."

General Akio swallowed hard. "Karza, you're to stay away from that man. Do I make myself clear?"

Anger flared in Karza's eyes, but Akio watched her get it under control before she answered. "As you say, General."

Akio heard the unspoken "for now" that Karza surely wanted to add to her answer.

****

Nori and Ruri watched the column of tanks as they roared along the street. Armed soldiers rode on their armored tops. The soldiers wore the grim expressions of men who were riding to their deaths. Nori was creeped out by the sight of them. She sat her drink down beside where she and Ruri sat on the edge of the road. Ruri was on her feet, snapping pictures of the tanks with her phone.

"This is so cool!" Ruri exclaimed as if she were a child watching a parade go by.

"Those are tanks, Ruri," Nori reminded her, trying to pull her friend back into reality.

"I know!" Ruri continued bouncing with excitement. "Something big is about to happen, and we're going to be a part of it. This could be the chance of a lifetime."

Nori sighed. Ruri was a journalism major with dreams of heading off to America when she finished her degree. With her love of crap like the stuff happening in front of them, Nori figured Ruri would be fantastic at it someday. The problem was Ruri was already doing it. She had her own blog and a small following that she played to every second of every day. It was more than a little annoying being forced to share her best friend with a faceless mass of internet groupies, but Nori supposed everyone had their cross to carry. She was a theology major herself. She had always loved religion and hoped there was something out there bigger than mankind and better than it was with all its greed, hate, and selfishness. Part of that she blamed on her father. The man hadn't been much of a father. Her mother had died when she was five, and instead of being there for her, the man had ended up in love with "the bottle." She was the one who tucked him in at night by the time she was seven. Nori would never forget the smell of alcohol on his breath and clothes when he would come home at night. The smell had always made her sick and still did. If not for the Australian missionary she had met when she was twelve, she might be just as messed up as her father had been and still was if truth be told. Jack was more than just a nice guy. He really believed what he preached and walked what he taught as best as any flawed human being could. Jack had taught her about grace and the love of God. At first, she hadn't wanted to believe, but then God had touched her heart. Never after that had she ever walked alone.

Nori loved Ruri like a sister, but she knew it was time to help her get a grip on herself before she did something that got them both in trouble. The soldiers were shooting dark glares at Ruri as she was snapping photos of them. Nori sighed and got to her feet.

"Ruri," she said putting a hand on her friend's shoulder. "I think you better stop that now."

Ruri spun around. "Stop what?"

"The pictures, Ruri," Nori told her cautiously. "Put up your phone, okay?"

"But I need some for my blog," Ruri protested. "This is the sort of stuff that makes you famous."

"There's a lot more to life than fame," Nori said and took the phone from Ruri.

"Hey!" Ruri shouted, reaching to take it back.

Nori pocketed the phone and shook her head. "Later. Something tells me we would be better off getting out of here while we still can."

Ruri stared at her as if she were crazy. "This is Tokyo, Nori, not a war zone."

"Take another look at those tanks, Ruri." Nori nodded in the direction of the column that was still passing by them. "From the looks of things, this city is about to become a warzone."

"Fine," Ruri huffed. "Classes are over for the day, so how do *you* want us to spend our evening?"

"Not chasing armed soldiers."

Ruri laughed. "You make that sound like it's a bad thing."

Nori ignored her. "Let's just get out of here, okay?"

Before Ruri could answer, the very ground they were standing on began to shake. Both girls wobbled on their legs trying to keep their balance.

"Earthquake!" they heard someone scream from across the street as panic erupted around them.

"What is that?" Ruri shrieked pointing up the street from where the two of them stood.

Nori whipped her head in the direction that Ruri was pointing to see the street breaking apart. It was being ripped apart from the shaking of the ground like one would expect to see from an earthquake, but rather it was being pushed upwards as it broke apart, as if something underneath it was forcing its way to the surface. Nori's eyes bugged as she saw it. The monster exploded from the ground, flopping the bulk of its putrid body onto the street. Its form was covered in coarse, thick, brown hair that was matted down by dirt and what smelt like sewer waste. Two blazing red orbs blazed above the elongated snout stretched outwards from its face. Its two front arm-like legs, or whatever they were, rested on the pavement, pushing down on it as it heaved the remainder of its body up from the hole it had opened in the street. All four of its strange arm-leg limbs ended in a trio of gleaming razor-like claws. The real horror set in as Nori realized it wasn't the only one of its kind. More creatures like it were emerging from the ground all around them. Nori could see a total of three of them from where she stood, frozen in place by utter shock.

Gunfire erupted from the soldiers riding on the tanks as they leapt into action. They hopped from the armored vehicles, rushing to engage the monsters. The rising cacophony of automatic weapons fire and the terrified screams of the other civilians on the street who were running for their lives snapped Nori into action herself. She grabbed a hold of Ruri from behind, catching her friend by surprise, and threw the two of them into the alley near where they had been standing on the street before everything went insane around them.

"My phone!" Ruri raged, clawing at Nori's pants pocket for it. "I need my phone!"

Nori could barely hear Ruri's shouts over the noise of the battle, and it truly was a battle now. The soldiers had encircled the beasts that had come up from the ground and were pouring everything they had into the creatures. Each of the strange beasts was over twenty feet long and stood a good eight feet high on their stubby built-for-digging legs. One of the beasts gave a grunt of pain as a grenade detonated under its belly, gutting it. With a sickening splash, its long strands of its intestines splattered onto the pavement. Another of the creatures charged the column of tanks plowing through and over the soldiers blocking its path. The soldiers were flung aside like dolls tossed by an angry child. They bounced off walls and rolled along the road in the creature's wake like broken toys. It was easy to see that many of them would never get up again. The main gun of the tank was turning, trying to come to bear on the creature, when it struck the tank. Armor crunched, folding inward, from the impact even before the stubby-legged monster rose itself up and began to swipe at the tank with its claws. They ripped the side of the tank open in a flurry of slashes almost too fast for Nori see.

Nori slapped Ruri's hands off of her. "Get it together, Ruri!" she screamed, not knowing if Ruri could hear her. "We've got to run!"

The tank the creature was tearing into exploded in a blossoming ball of flame that flashed outward even as it streaked upwards towards the heavens. The fire engulfed the creature and several of the soldiers who unlucky enough to be near the tank when it went up. The shockwave from the explosion slammed into Nori and Ruri, knocking them from their feet.

Nori went down hard but managed to twist her body at just the right angle to avoid being too badly hurt by the fall. Ruri met the ground with her face. Nori scrambled back to her feet as

Ruri looked up at her. Tears streamed from Ruri's eyes, and her nose was a mess of mangled meat and running blood.

Cupping a hand over her mouth, Nori tried not to scream at the sight of her friend's face. She honestly couldn't even believe that Ruri was still conscious after taking a hard blow. Nori got control of her emotions, saying a silent prayer for strength, and took Ruri by the hand, helping her to stand.

The battle was still raging outside the mouth of the alley Nori had managed to get the two of them into. The sound of gunfire remained constant, though it sounded like there were less guns being fired. The sharp, distinct chattering of a turret-mounted machine gun from one of the tanks more than made up for it, though. It was louder than even the ringing that already filled Nori's ears.

Ruri tried to speak, but her words were too mumbled and distorted for Nori to understand. One of Ruri's pupils was larger than the other. Nori knew that was bad. There was a hospital just a few blocks away, so that's where Nori decided to try for. She helped Ruri get an arm up and onto her, around her shoulder, so that she could support part of Ruri's weight and the two of them hobbled away from the battle without looking back.

****

Two Kawasaki OH-1 helicopters came streaking across the sky at speeds in excess of two hundred miles an hour. Captain

Orto was in command aboard the Katana. The Katana's sister, the Shrike, was being flown by Gushi, a long-time flight partner of Orto's. The OH-1s were nicknamed Ninjas and with good reason. Their capacity for surgical strike-level fire was dead on, and that was exactly what was called for here in the streets of Tokyo. There were scattered civilians everywhere, trapped inside the combat zone, where the fifth column was engaged with two monsters that had apparently crawled out of the depths of Hell itself.

Captain Orto had a difficult time believing what he was seeing with his own eyes. He had stories of real kaiju but never had imagined such things could truly be real. Kaiju was the only name to describe the two abominations, though. They resembled overgrown and deformed garden moles. Two of them were among the tanks of the fifth column, tearing the great armored vehicles apart with the massive claws of their hands (or were they feet?). The corpse of a third smoldered nearby next to the blown-out hull of an MBT Type 10. Orto was glad he was well above the battle; even so, the phantom smell of burning meat and hair made his stomach twist up inside of him.

"Weapons hot," Gushi informed him over the comm. link the two copters shared.

"Time to send these things back where they came from," Orto acknowledged with a ferocious grin parting his lips. "Just be careful of the tanks."

The Type 91 surface-to-air missiles the two Ninjas carried were perfect for the job and all the tanks closest to the two monsters were long dead. Captain Orto and Gushi had arrived at a nearly perfect time for their strike. Now, they just had to hit the monsters before the things managed to close on the rest of the fifth column.

"Fire on my mark," Captain Orto ordered as the engines of the two Ninjas howled, and they descended on a strafing run that aimed the noses of the two copters directly at the monsters.

Orto waited for only of a fraction of second before giving the order. "Fire!"

Two missiles left each of the Ninjas, blasting forth from their pods, to go blazing ahead of the helicopters. The first pair struck the larger of the two kaiju moles. It blew apart like a rotten melon as the explosion flung chunks of its body into the air in a rain of blood and splintering bone. The smaller of the two kaiju moles, unlike its companion, saw the missiles aimed for it coming. It tried to heave its heavy body out of their flight path at the last moment but was just too slow. Its death was instantaneous as the missiles. Orto imagined the tips of the missiles stabbing into the great beast like primitive spears before the monster vanished in a flash of light in front of him. He jerked on his controls, pulling his Ninja up hard back into the sky. Gushi's bird followed him.

"This is Katana I," Captain Orto reported over the comm. of his helmet. "The kaiju have been eliminated. Katana I and Katana II—returning to base."

Captain Orto wished every mission were as easy as this one had been. He'd heard of what happened to General Akio's fleet as it had been in route for Tokyo and mumbled a prayer of thanks that the kaiju he had been sent to engage were nothing like those things were reported to have been like.

****

"Well, that was unexpected," General Akio commented, handing the report back to his aide and advisor, Heather Karza. "Did we know kaiju like that even existed?"

Karza huffed at him. "There are apparently no limits to what kaiju can be. The attack of those moles things have stirred up all of Tokyo. The entire city is in a panic."

"Nothing to be done about it now except declare martial law."

"Which is what I had recommended from the moment the tanks starting entering the city," Karza reminded him.

"So you did," General Akio acknowledged. "What do you want from me, Karza? You were right, I was wrong. Does that make you feel any better? Does it help us with the situation we currently have?"

"No," Karza answered in a surprisingly calm voice. "No, sir, it doesn't. I will pass along the order and get things as under control as we can with the forces we have at hand. Most of the troops, outside of those in this building, are already assigned to the city's defense force and in position to engage the kaiju upon the arrival of the monsters."

"These kaiju moles," General Akio stopped Karza before she could scurry away, "do we know we there are more of them?"

"Not at this time," Karza told him. "We are setting up seismograph equipment in hopes of being able to determine just that."

"Good," General Akio sighed. "We need to strongly consider what other kinds of kaiju are out there that we might not see coming as well."

"Trust me, I am, sir," Karza assured him. "If you'll excuse me, though, I have an entire city of panicked civilians to get under control."

****

Commander Hiroto stood on the bridge of the DESRON Samurai II's flagship. Long-range sonar had detected numerous inbound contacts half an hour earlier. The contacts were moving slowly towards the position that his DESRON and the American carrier group designated Task force Gamma Red had taken up just off the coast. All the ships of both groups were on high alert. In fact, the American Admiral Hall had scrambled the bulk of his available air wing. The sky was full of F-16s, F-18s, and even a small group of bombers. Two Seahawk copters circled the joint formation under Hiroto's command. Hiroto wasn't exactly comfortable giving the American admiral orders and tried to keep the two of them at least on the appearance of an equal level of power. The American outranked him, but this was a Japanese op. in Japanese waters, and the American had agreed after all to render aid as needed.

Tearing his thoughts away from the American admiral, Hiroto turned his attention back to the inbound contacts. It bothered him greatly that were approaching at such a casual pace, as if they were totally unconcerned of the joint military force in their path. None of the sonar techs had been able to put a true number on the contacts. The readings were too distorted. At best, three large kaiju were approaching. At worst, it was an entire army of lesser ones. The lesser Kaiju seemed a greater threat by Hiroto's standards. The large monsters were usually easily detectable and even easier targets. Yes, they were more difficult to kill, but with them, at least one knew where they stood. If even one of the odd sonar readings represented a group of lesser kaiju, it could break apart as it closed on the joint task force and swarm it. Not even the American ships were designed to fight an army of fast, agile monsters attempting to board them.

Hiroto sighed and took a seat in his command chair as his XO sauntered up to him.

"Should we open fire on the contacts, sir?"

Hiroto shook his head. "Not yet, John."

American names were growing more common in Japan but Hiroto, even after two years of working together, almost had to stifle a laugh every time he called his XO by his first name.

"Let those things get just a little closer, John," Hiroto ordered.

"What if the Americans—?"

"The Americans won't fire until we do, unless something changes," Hiroto interrupted. "Admiral Hall is well aware that I am in command here."

"As you say, sir," John replied. "Are the kaiju still CBDR?"

CBDR in naval terms meant constant bearing, decreasing range.

"Sir!" Hiroto's sonar tech shouted across the bridge at him. "The kaiju are increasing speed!"

"Well, I guess that answers that," Hiroto snorted. "Report!"

"One of the contacts has broken up, sir. It's become hundreds, maybe more, a clear reading on it is impossible. All of them are inbound for the American carrier."

"And the other two contacts?" Hiroto demanded.

"They're coming our way, sir. Their speed has increased to over 30 knots!"

"Heaven have mercy," Hiroto heard his XO mutter. "That's ramming speed!"

There was no more time for Hiroto to worry about the Americans. The larger kaiju were streaking towards the ships under his command.

"All ships of Samurai II, take the inbound contacts with guns!" Hiroto shouted over the open channel to the rest of the Japanese DESRON. "Fire at will! I repeat, fire at will!"

His flagship, the *Yakaze,* opened up on the kaiju first. Torpedoes slipped into the waves from her tubes, darting towards the giant monsters. The *Tachikaze, Noakaze,* and *Akikaze* followed suit. Cannons thundered and missile launchers spat volley after volley. In the midst of the churning water and explosions, the two kaiju slowed. One of them appeared hurt, given how it moved on the sonar screen of the *Yakaze.* It rolled beneath the water and disappeared. The other kaiju remained stationary until the barrage of fire came to a halt, as the ships of Samurai II had no choice but to wait for their armaments to be loaded or cycle up new ammo. As soon as the pause in the firing came, the kaiju hurled itself forward again.

"The remaining kaiju has increased its speed to over 40 knots, sir!" Hiroto's sonar tech informed him.

"Evasive maneuvers!" Hiroto screamed, but he knew it was too late.

The kaiju burst from the water. Its upper body was like a human's except that it was covered in reptilian scales. Its head was like that of a squid's, conical and pointed. Impossibly large, yellow eyes stretched down each of the sides of that head. The massive claws of the fingers of its left hand raked the side of the *Tachikaze* from bow to stern with the terrible sound of rending metal. Its right hand slammed into the *Noakaze* at mid-ship. The *Noakaze* was knocked over onto her side, nearly breaking apart at the point of impact.

Hiroto could hear the captain of the *Tachikaze* giving the order to abandon ship. From the *Noakaze*, there was only muffled, screaming voices that filled the airwaves. Hiroto knew the *Noakaze* was lost. The kaiju's punch had lifted the destroyer and flung it through the air before it came down hard on its side. Even now, the ship was continuing to split along its middle. Inwardly, he prayed for any who were still alive aboard it.

The *Akikaze* unloaded a volley of missiles into the squid kaiju's back. Explosions peppered the kaiju as it moved closer to the *Tachikaze*, taking hold of the destroyer with both its hands. The squid kaiju swung the *Tachikaze* around through the water into the *Akikaze*. Both ships vanished in a flash of light that made Hiroto shield his eyes and turn away from the blast.

In its wake, the kaiju was howling, its head reared back in pain. Both of its hands were gone. The ends of its arms were little more than bloody stumps. The death of the *Tachikaze* and *Akikaze* had cost the kaiju far more than the great beast had counted on.

"Fire!" Hiroto found himself shouting at his weapons officer. "Fire!"

The squid kaiju was close enough to the *Yakaze* now that the ship's C.I.W.S. had sprung to life and engaged it. High-velocity rounds hammered into the kaiju at a rate of three thousand rounds a minute. They ripped away at its already-injured flesh. The squid kaiju was a mess. Burns and grooves of bullet-torn scales covered it. Black blood leaked from its body in rivers that ran into the ocean water around it.

Every weapon that *Yakaze* had available that could target the wounded squid kaiju opened up on the monster. Tracer rounds streaked the air between the monster and the flagship of Samurai II. Missiles blew away chunks of the monster's right shoulder. A volley of near point-blank torpedoes ruptured the already-weakened armor scales covering its guts. The squid kaiju's cries

54

ended as it collapsed, mid-lunge for *Yakaze*. The tip of its head sliced the port side of the destroyer as the great beast flopped about in its death throes.

The bridge crew of the *Yakaze* were tossed and flung about both by the impact of the tip of the kaiju's skull and the shockwave of the thing's massive body splashing down onto the surface of the ocean. As the kaiju's body sank, the *Yakaze* was jerked about on the waves.

The *Yakaze*'s helm blew out in a shower of sparks that set the helmsman ablaze. He screamed as he threw himself from his chair, rolling about on the metal floor of the bridge. Other stations blew, sections of the ceiling came crashing down to bury panicked crewmen. The forward window shattered, sending a hail of glass shards slicing into those who were still on their feet. Hiroto had managed to remain in his command chair, clinging to it for dear life. He was there when a piece of the forward window struck him. It entered his skull through the right side of his head, slicing away the top of his ear in the process. Hiroto's life ended in a bright flash of pain before his body toppled from his chair to thud onto the floor. The part of the shard of glass protruding from the side of his head gleamed in the red emergency lighting of the bridge.

****

The air wing of Task force Gamma Red would have been engaging the kaiju that went after the ships of the Japanese DESRON, Samurai II, but they had their own problems. As the two large kaiju laid waste to Samurai II and the ships of Task force Gamma Red fought for their lives against an army of lesser kaiju which had risen from the depths, the air wing itself had also come under attack. The kaiju, somehow completely invisible to radar, had swept down upon the fighters of the air wing without warning. One moment, there were six F-16s and nine F-18s soaring over the unfolding battle, and in the next second, more than half of that force was gone. The bird-like *things* descended upon the fighters like monstrous banshees. Their shrieks were so loud that they actually played havoc with the electronics of the fighters, blowing out canopy covers and sensitive internal circuit boards. They nosedived into the F-16s and F-18s, plowing through them. The wreckage of broken fighters rained into the ocean, leaving fiery trails of smoke across the sky in their wake.

"Break hard!" Captain Martin of Eagle Squadron yelled.

Already, the remaining fighters of Eagle, Hawk, and Falcon Squadrons were doing so. F-16s and F-18s rolled through the clouds, abandoning their formations.

Falcon 2 veered right, dodging one of the bird creatures that came sweeping at it. Henderson, Falcon 2's pilot, punched it, speeding away from the kaiju. It angled around to chase after him.

"Got one on my tail!" Henderson shouted. "Little help here, guys!"

"Hold on Falcon 2," Captain Martin said, trying to keep his voice calm, "I'm on my way!"

Captain Martin had counted at least two dozen of the bird kaiju so far. He had no idea if that accounted for all the creatures or if there were more outside his field of vision. Whatever the birds were doing to make themselves undetectable by his fighter's gear, they were still doing it. And the bird kaiju certainly had the advantage. Their unexpected attack had left the squadrons of the air wing in utter chaos.

Eagle 1 slipped into position behind the kaiju chasing Falcon 2 as Captain Martin tried to get a lock on it. His F-16's targeting system refused to even acknowledge that the kaiju existed. Captain Martin saw he was going to have to do things the old-fashioned way. The forward guns of his F-16 spat streams of fire at the kaiju. They raked over the kaiju's back and wings. The kaiju swerved to the left and plummeted from the sky in a downward spin. Falcon 2 was in the clear.

Eagle 1 and Falcon 2 arched around on a course back towards where the rest of their squadrons fought for their lives against the kaiju. Falcon 4 became a blossoming cloud of flames, smoke, and shrapnel as one of the kaiju crashed directly into it. The kaiju didn't appear to care if they lived or died so long as they took at least one fighter with them. Captain Martin didn't know what to make of such insane tactics, but that was something he could think about later if he managed to survive the next few minutes.

Falcon 6 fired two missiles from its wings. They blazed through the air, streaking towards one of the kaiju. The kaiju saw them coming. It opened its deformed monstrosity of a beak to let loose a shriek that had an effect like that of a sonic cannon on the inbound missiles. They exploded in flight still far from it. The move, however, left the kaiju holding nearly stationary, as the beast had needed to kill its forward momentum. Captain Martin took advantage of that coming in hard and fast at the kaiju. Missiles from his own fighter's wings roared ahead of him. The missiles slammed into the kaiju, blowing its body apart. Eagle 1 flew straight through the mess of splattered flesh the kaiju had been reduced to. When he emerged on the other side, Captain Martin spotted Eagle 4. Eagle 4 was maneuvering hard to avoid a kaiju that was determined to sink its talons into it.

The kaiju was bearing down on Eagle 4 as Eagle 1 approached it from its right side. Captain Martin laid into the monster with Eagle 1's cannons. The heavy rounds dug huge holes in the beast's sides. It squawked and hurled itself away from Eagle 1's line of fire. The kaiju was gravely injured and tried to break away from the engagement raging around it. Captain Martin refused to let the monster go.

Eagle 1 closed on the wounded kaiju, its engines being pushed to their limits, as Captain Martin fired another two missiles. The wounded kaiju didn't have a prayer for avoiding them, hurt as it was. They made contact with the kaiju's back as they exploded, turning the kaiju into a mess of charred and exploding flesh.

Captain Martin allowed himself a smile. It quickly twisted into an expression of grim determination driven by fear as he saw Eagle 1 was the sole survivor of the *Lee*'s air wing that was still in the sky. Everyone else was gone. His quick look around also told him that at least six of the kaiju remained in play, and *all* of them were now coming after him. It was unbelievable that such creatures could take out an air wing, much less so quickly, but they had.

Alarms sounded in the cockpit of his fighter signaling that one Eagle 1's engines had just gone offline. Captain Martin knew he had pushed them too hard. As Eagle 1 lurched in the sky and he adjusted his heading to help compensate for the lack of power, the kaiju overtook him. The last thing Captain Martin saw before he died was the talons of a massive foot closing over the canopy of his fighter above. He barely even had time to scream.

****

The *Lee*'s C.I.W.S. was going wild attempting to engage all the lesser kaiju surrounding the ship. Wherever its stream of fire intercepted the hordes of kaiju, the creatures died by the dozens. It wasn't enough, though. There was simply too many of the things.

Admiral Hall had ordered Colonel Stockholm and all available personnel to arm themselves. If the kaiju managed to get into the ship's interior, all was lost. There would be no stopping them. The plan was to stop them before they ever had the chance to do so. It was up to Stockholm to make sure that happened. He sent marines and ready-action teams accompanied by personnel who were normally noncombatants to every exterior deck of the *Lee*. Stockholm led the team who were attempting to hold the main deck himself.

Gunfire rang out all around Stockholm as his men got into position. Two of them, who were carrying S.A.W.s, did their best to hold the bulk of the kaiju at bay. Each of the kaiju was different from the others. All of them, though, stood between seven and nine feet tall. Some had legs, others moved about on two primary tentacles that functioned as legs. Stockholm even saw a few who had lower bodies that resembled snakes who came slithering across the deck towards their prey. And that's what Stockholm felt he and his men were—prey. Whenever one of the *Lee*'s defenders fell, numerous kaiju piled onto the body, ripping away it with their teeth and claws.

"Hey ugly!" Stockholm called at a group of kaiju who were devouring the remains of a lieutenant he thought had been named Haney. Three of the seven kaiju raised their heads, their burning eyes turning in his direction. Two of them had chunks of Haney in their mouths as they did so.

The goat-horned head of one of the kaiju in the group around Haney that had looked up burst as Stockholm put three rounds from his M-16A into the thing's skull. Its body careened over backwards, thudding onto the deck. The other kaiju left Haney's body where it lay to charge towards him. A communications tech, drafted into the defense of the ship, moved up beside Stockholm as the colonel made his stand. The tech clutched a 9mm in a two-handed grip and was busy emptying the weapon's mag. into the kaiju even as Stockholm flicked his M-16A to automatic and held down its trigger. Their combined fire tore the group of kaiju apart before they got within six feet of where Stockholm and the tech stood.

The battle was going badly. Stockholm could already see that it was lost. There were already hundreds of the lesser kaiju already aboard the *Lee* and more continued to scale the sides of the ship with each passing minute. Stockholm heard one of the two S.A.W.s nearby jam and go silent. The soldier who had been firing it cursed loudly before a kaiju that resembled a cross between a chicken and jellyfish of all things engulfed the soldier in its tentacles. The S.A.W. clattered to the deck as the soldier died from the creature's stings, his flesh swelling and splitting even as he jerked about in the creature's grasp. The soldier with the other S.A.W. turned to vaporize the kaiju with a stream of point-blank fire. The jellyfish kaiju exploded in a shower of black ooze and pulp.

Stockholm heard the tech next to him grunt. He whirled to see the horn of a kaiju protruding through the man's sternum. The kaiju rose to its full height as it flung the dead tech off of it. The kaiju towered over Stockholm, easily standing nine feet tall. Stockholm didn't even blink. He just pointed the barrel of his M-16A at the creature and blasted it with a trio of three-round bursts. The kaiju went staggering backwards to topple onto the deck. It was a good bet that monster wasn't dead, but Stockholm's attention was torn from it by some idiot shouting, "Fall back!"

There was nowhere to fall back to. The kaiju had overrun the exterior decks of the destroyer and surrounded the position he and most of the others were still trying to hold. Stockholm wanted to shoot the idiot who had yelled the order but had no idea who it was in the crowd. Besides, the three of his men who had turned to run had been cut down by the kaiju as soon as they had left the relative security of the tightened circle his other men had formed.

Each one of his men who fell took several of the lesser kaiju with them, and the soldier with S.A.W. was still proving to worth his weight in gold, but even so, it was just a matter of time until all of them were dead himself included.

A kaiju with four arms, each of which was more like a blade than a true arm, leaped into the circle of the *Lee*'s defenders, slashing wildly. One man howled as the monster severed his spine from behind him. Another lost his head to a quick swipe of one of the monster's arms. The monster slid its third arm deep into the side of a soldier who had managed to halfway turn towards it. It twisted the blade about inside the man's body, showing rows of long, razor-like teeth in a feral, gleeful grin as it did, too. Its fourth arm stabbed at Stockholm. He managed to block the thrust with his rifle. The weapon was ruined in the process, but the act saved his life.

Stockholm's hand tore a grenade from where it dangled on the side of his belt. He pulled its pin with his teeth as his other hand drew his sidearm from the holster on his hip. Stockholm's pistol cracked over and over as he emptied half the pistol's magazine in the four-armed kaiju's mouth and eyes.

He was alone now. Stockholm could hear distant gunfire from other parts of the ship, but the men near him were all dead. As the kaiju closed in on him, he smashed the live grenade into the chest of the closest one. He felt his hand be torn apart by the blast at the point of impact before shrapnel from the grenade slammed into him and all the kaiju around him.

****

Admiral Hall, his helmsman, and the *Lee*'s communications officer were the only people left on the bridge. Hall had sent everyone else to engage and try to stop the endless waves lesser kaiju that were still swarming onto the ship. The *Lee*'s C.I.W.S. had long fallen silent. An armored kaiju that resembled a beetle had crawled its way to the weapon and taken it out, ripping it from its emplacement and throwing it over the side of the ship into the water.

The door to the bridge was sealed and welded shut. It wouldn't hold long, though. Already Hall could hear the fists of the frenzied kaiju on its other side slamming into it with all their strength. The door buckled in its frame, metal bending inward.

"Sir," Jake, the ship's helmsman said, trying to get his attention.

Hall looked at the man, half-dazed. It took a moment for him to realize that Jake was offering him his sidearm. Bridge officers weren't supposed to be armed, but Hall had everyone he could get armed before the lesser kaiju had attacked the ship in force.

Taking the weapon, Hall nodded his thanks. "You armed?" he asked the communications officer.

She shook her head in the negative. "No, sir. Didn't think I would need to be."

"We need to get out of here, sir," Jake urged him. "That door is going to give any second."

"There's no point in running, Jake," Hall told him in a sad voice. "This ship belongs to those monsters now. There's nowhere to run to."

The look Jake shot at him made it clear that the helmsman regretted giving him his weapon.

"Look!" the communications officer screamed, pointing at the forward window.

Admiral Hall and Jake turned to see its glass was covered in the bodies of kaiju with sucker-like hands. The monsters were attached to the window and using their dome-shaped heads like hammers trying to crack it. They were succeeding, too. Hall wondered if there was any end to the number of abominations contained in the kaiju's ranks.

The bridge door came flying inward. The kaiju trying to push through it had actually knocked it loose from its frame and sent it spiraling, end over end. The poor communications officer was caught between the door and her console. She died like a cartoon character crushed by a dropped piano. *The only difference,* Hall thought, *was the amount of blood.*

Jake had no weapon but charged to meet the kaiju anyway. He died instantly as the mandibles of an ant-headed kaiju caught and closed about his neck. Jake's head bounced off the bridge's deck a few times before rolling to a stop in the bridge's far corner.

Admiral Hall thought about shoving the 9mm pistol in his hand into his mouth and squeezing its trigger before the kaiju reached him. He didn't, though. It would have been a dishonor to the men and women he had led into this fight. Hall brought the pistol up and managed to fire a single shot that splattered the ant-headed kaiju's skull before the rest of the kaiju swept over him, knocking him to the floor beneath them. His screams echoed off the walls of the bridge as clawed fingers, pincers, and teeth shredded his flesh until he lay unmoving in a pool of his own blood.

****

Lieutenant Sam Worley and his tactical officer, Harper, were having a really crappy day. Harper sat beside him in the copilot seat while Ensign Carpenter manned the cabin door mounted M60D. Worley was thankful for the sound suppressant aspect of his flight helmet as Carpenter continued to hammer away with the weapon at the kaiju that ran amok over the *Lee*'s exterior decks. It was easy to see that the carrier was lost. They would have been dead, too, had he not ordered the others aboard the Seahawk and managed to get the bird into the air before the kaiju overran the last of the carrier's rapid response teams of marines. The other Seahawk the *Lee* carried was now a burning pile of wreckage upon the flight deck.

Worley and his crew had attempted to provide support for the troops attempting to defend the carrier but not even adding their firepower had proved enough. The kaiju's numbers were just too great. He and his crew had watched as the last of the carrier's defenders had formed a tight circle in the middle of the flight deck and tried to stand their ground. The battle hadn't lasted long at all, and now those men were dead. Worley had allowed Carpenter to vent some of her anger on the monsters, even after the last of the soldiers below fell, but now it was time to move on.

The destroyers of Task force Gamma Red hadn't fared any better than the *Lee* had. All of the ships of the American force they belonged to were nothing more than swarms of rampaging kaiju. And the ships of the Japanese DESRON they had been assisting were shattered messes of flaming wreckage that burned brightly as they drifted upon the waves.

"What in the devil do we do now, Sam?" Harper asked.

Worley didn't have an answer to that question. So far, the winged kaiju that had decimated the F-16s and F-18s of the *Lee*'s air wing had left them alone. In truth, Worley had no idea where the winged monsters had vanished to once they had finished with the fighters. He doubted they had left the area. Most likely, the things were high above their Seahawk, hiding in the clouds, somewhere. Maybe the monsters deemed that a lone copter was below their attention, or perhaps they were just waiting for the right moment to come swooping down on it. There was no way to know for sure.

Worley shook his head. "Head for Tokyo," he said. "That's all we can do. If we stay here, we're dead like everyone else."

"Hey, Carpenter!" Harper shouted on the trio's shared comm. link. "Cool with it the M60! The last thing we want right now is to draw attention to this bird!"

The M60 fell silent in the copter's rear as Carpenter answered, "Roger that."

"Tokyo then," Harper said, nodding towards the horizon.

Worley pushed the Seahawk's engines to their max as the copter flew across the sky, leaving the *Lee* behind it.

****

Colonel Yuri was the onsite CO for the columns of armored vehicles and tanks that lined the docks of Tokyo harbor. There were reports coming in that the joint American/Japanese naval task force had been destroyed by the kaiju approaching the city. That meant any minute now, it would be up to him and his men to do what the Navy had failed to do. General Akio's orders were clear. There could be no retreat no matter how the battle went.

Night had fallen, and the docks were lit by huge searchlights, their beams panning out across the waves of the harbor. All that could be done was to wait for the kaiju to come. The wait was not a long one.

The kaiju rose from the water. There were four of the monsters in all, each of them was a horrid abomination that writhed above the waves, their bodies the shape of snakes. At least that was what Colonel Yuri thought at first. His jaw fell open in shock and terror as the kaiju continued to rise and he saw that what he had thought were four different kaiju were, in reality, the heads of a single monster. When it had risen to its full height, its snake-like heads above its body, the kaiju towered a good four hundred feet high. Two heads hissed, one reared back giving a vicious roar, while the fourth was silent, its mouth filled with crackling blue energy that danced and flashed over the rows of its fanged teeth.

"All units, fire at will!" Colonel Yuri shouted.

The tanks lining the docks rocked the night with fire from their main guns. The sound was like a chorus of thunder as a barrage of shells rocketed towards the kaiju. Explosions rippled all over the kaiju's chest. Rounds designed to pierce the heaviest of armor did little more than gouge at the thick scales that passed for the kaiju's skin. The secondary weapons of the tanks joined in, orange tracer rounds slashing through the night as bullets poured into the kaiju by the thousands.

Colonel Yuri saw that the massive kaiju had no arms but two thick legs supported the monster's body as it waded towards the docks. Its wide, rounded body swayed beneath the amount of firepower his tanks were hitting it with. Even so, it came onward. Its fourth head struck first. It shot forward like a striking snake to unleash a bolt of blue lightning. The bolt hit not one but two tanks that were close together in the defensive formation that lined the docks. The energy danced over their armored hulls like a raging electrical storm. Colonel Yuri heard the last cries of those two tank crews as they were cooked alive inside their vehicles.

The two hissing heads struck next. Their mouths opened as they hosed the docks with wide cones of fire so hot that the armor of the tanks the fire made contact with turned to slag. Metal melted, running like candle wax to pool around the now misshapen remnants of the tanks. The destruction those two heads inflicted in their initial attack was devastating, half a dozen tanks lost in mere seconds.

The roaring head struck last. Colonel Yuri could see bulges working their way up its throat to its mouth like there was something alive inside the kaiju that was pushing out of it. When the roaring head opened its mouth, it spat boulder after boulder towards the docks. The huge rocks crushed the tanks they hit, but they did far more than that. They shook the docks themselves as their weight came crashing down them. Entire sections of the docks broke apart, dumping the heart of Colonel Yuri's battle line into the water. Yuri could see that the huge rocks had been swallowed by the kaiju earlier, and the beast was now vomiting them up as weapons to be hurled at its enemies. He knew the kaiju couldn't possibly have that many more of the rocks inside it, but he couldn't chance another attack like the one his tanks had just been hit by.

"Get those tanks off the docks!" Yuri raged at the closest officer to him before he addressed his men himself over his unit's comm. link. "Keep firing but fall back! I say again, fall back!"

The tanks still able to respond to his orders began the slow process of a backwards retreat, even as they continued to hammer the kaiju. The kaiju was beginning to show the effects of their constant barrage. Areas of the monster's scales had been blown away, and black pus oozed from those wounds into the water around its legs. Though Yuri could see dozens of such wounds on the kaiju's chest and upper legs, none were bad enough or deep enough to truly slow the kaiju down. It lumbered on towards the remains of the docks and the city of Tokyo beyond them.

The two heads that had spat fire and the electrical head all struck again in unison, decimating another third of Colonel Yuri's remaining forces as his tanks did their best to clear the docks and regroup on the solid ground behind them. Yuri knew he had to come up with something and fast. He needed a means to hurt the kaiju more and slow it or soon he wouldn't have any tanks under his command left.

"All surviving battle capable units, aim for that thing's heads!" Yuri shouted. "We need to take them out before they take us out!"

Yuri was cursing loudly even as his tanks began to concentrate their fire on the kaiju's heads. Where in the devil is my air support? he wondered. General Akio should have had plenty of time by now to scramble whatever fighters or copters that were on standby in the area.

The concentrating of the fire on the heads worked to a degree. Six tanks trained their main guns on one of the hissing, fire-breathing heads. Their shells blew chunks of flesh away from its face that spun through the air, flinging black blood as they went. One of the tanks got lucky. Its shell actually landed inside the head's mouth and detonated there. Colonel Yuri saw the eyes of the head burst from their sockets to dangle by strands of sinew on the sides of the head's face. The head bucked about wildly, before the strength of its neck muscles gave out, and it flopped to bounce against the scales of the kaiju's chest, hanging there limply and clearly dead.

Shouts of triumph and excitement filled the unit's communications net. Even Colonel Yuri allowed himself a smile. It was a start at stopping the giant monster and a sorely needed one. Yuri's smile vanished as the kaiju's remaining three heads all cried out, and the monster picked up its pace. The earthshaking strides of its thick legs quickened as the monster all-out charged the cluster of remaining tanks between it and the city of Tokyo.

Colonel Yuri braced himself for the end as the kaiju neared the position of the APC he was using as his command center. The tanks had fallen back to gather around it as a rallying point in their retreat. The end didn't come, however. A wave of fighters came howling in over his APC and the tanks on a direct course for the kaiju. Their forward cannons were already blazing as missiles leapt from the launchers on the underside of their wings. The missiles stabbed at the kaiju's central mass like spears, their explosions digging deep into the already-weakened armor of its scales. Their impact brought the kaiju to a dead stop, ending its charge.

The kaiju was far from out of the fight, though. One of the monster's heads lashed out, catching a fighter in its teeth. The plane exploded there as those teeth ground into it, tearing it apart. The blast was a flash of blinding light as all the plane's fuel and remaining missiles went up at once. There wasn't much left of the head that had grabbed the plane afterwards. The neck supporting the mangled mass of burnt meat that had once been the roaring head of the kaiju went limp and flopped downward to dangle beside the beast's other destroyed head. The kaiju was reeling about now like a drunken man. Its steps were awkward and ill placed, barely keeping the great beast upright.

A crackling bolt of blue energy took out another of the fighters as they sped passed the kaiju. The sole remaining fighter didn't swing about to engage the kaiju again. Instead, it veered away from the great beast, making a run for it. Colonel Yuri understood that fighters pilot didn't want to die, but neither did his men. Shaking his fist at the fleeing plane, Yuri slid down from the turret he had been watching the battle from into the APC that was his command center. Even as he was sealing it above him, he was barking orders to the commanders of his tanks.

"Keep concentrating on the heads! We've almost got this thing!" he yelled.

Shells flew to slam into the kaiju's two heads that were still dangerous, and this time, they were just enough to bring down the beast. It rocked back and forth on its legs before it took a final step and collapsed forward. Unfortunately for Colonel Yuri, the kaiju had closed enough space for its body to fall directly onto the most forward tanks of the new formation his forces had retreated into and on top of his own APC as well.

The roof above Colonel Yuri bent inward, crushing down upon him. His scream became a sickening, gargling noise as he and the APC he was in were flattened by the kaiju's weight.

****

Captain Eito suddenly found himself in command with Colonel Yuri and most of the other ranking officers either dead or at least unresponsive to the chaos of desperate voices crying out over the unit's communications net. Eito smacked the wall of the tank next to him as he shouted for his driver to throw the tank into reverse. He quickly ordered all the remaining units to report their status. Five other tanks and one APC answered, reporting that they were battle capable. *Five tanks out of three dozen,* Eito thought as his stomach twisted up in knots. *So many dead, so fast.*

"All units, Colonel Yuri is dead. This is Captain Eito of the *Battle-Hardened*. I am assuming overall command of this unit."

Eito paused for a moment to allow his words to sink in before he continued. "I want all units to fire two more rounds each into that thing out there! We can't afford it getting up again."

The body of the kaiju didn't so much as flinch as the new barrage of fire ripped away at its scales. Eito nodded inside his tank, admitting to himself that the monster must surely be dead.

"This is the *Honor-Bound!*" Eito heard one of the other tank commanders shouting over the comm. "We've got new incoming from the ocean, sir!"

"All units, maneuver around this thing's body to get a clear shot at the water. We've got more kaiju inbound!"

Eito's half-formed hope that the battle might be over died as he saw the swarms of lesser kaiju rushing up the beach. There were more of them than he could count, maybe thousands. On the upside, as terrifying as the monsters looked, none of them were that much larger than man-sized.

"The worst is over," Eito assured the others. "The big one is down. We *have* to hold these little bastards, though. We're all that's left between them and Tokyo!"

"Roger, Roger!"

"Read you loud and clear, Captain!"

"On it!"

"Die, you little…!"

Eito smiled as he heard the others reporting in and confirming his orders. The *Battle-Hardened* lurched on her threads as her main gun fired, hurling a shell into the ranks of the charging kaiju. Bits and pieces of kaiju bodies flew skyward around the shell's point of impact. The main guns of the other tanks were thundering, too. Explosions raked the beach, killing entire packs of the lesser kaiju. The kaiju kept coming, though, oblivious to their brothers and sisters dying around them as they charged forward.

Two of the remaining tanks had lost their secondary weapons, but those that still had functional machine guns let loose on the kaiju, even as the tanks' main guns continued to fire. Kaiju fell like wheat struck down by a farmer's scythe wherever the orange flashes of tracer rounds guided the tanks' fire.

"Holy…those little buggers are fast!" Eito heard one of his fellow commanders shouting.

And then the lesser kaiju were on them. The monsters ran up to the tanks, slashing at them with claws that shredded the metal hulls. Others of the kaiju spat streams of a greenish liquid that burned like acid. Still others scampered up onto the tops of the tanks and began to try to tear their way into them to reach their crews.

The gunner in the cupola of Eito's tank, above him, died as greenish, glowing acid melted the flesh from his bones. Drops of it sprayed onto Eito, even as he tried to duck deeper inside the tank to avoid it. The drops that hit him smoldered on the sleeves of his jacket as they ate through it to touch his skin. Eito screamed as he looked at his arms to see the newly formed holes through his flesh and bone alike.

The kaiju that had killed the gunner grabbed the man's smoking corpse and flung it aside to ram its head down into Eito's tank. Eito's eye went wide as it came face to face with him in the enclosed space. Despite his pain, he struggled to draw the pistol holstered on his hip. Before he could, though, the kaiju opened its mouth and a stream of glowing green washed over him.

****

"We're getting slaughtered out there, Akio," Karza growled at him.

General Akio couldn't argue with her assessment of the current situation. Both the joint Japanese/American naval task force and the armored divisions he had placed in the city's harbor had failed to stop the kaiju. He still had plenty of infantry in the city and had held back most of his air forces in reserve, but even so, he had been in enough battles over the years to know they were royally and totally screwed.

"It's time to go after Director Diasuke, and you know it...sir," Karza made the last word sound like an insult.

"Agreed," General Akio admitted solemnly. "We have failed. It's also time to evacuate the city, no matter what may come of such an order."

The powers above Akio and Karza had given them carte blanche over the city and whatever forces they needed to defend it just to prevent such an order from being given. There would be Hell to pay for them both later if they survived the night.

"Get the car ready," General Akio ordered. "This is something that we should do in person."

"We?" Karza asked, surprised.

"Yes, we," General Akio replied. "Things may get a bit...rough, and I want you there."

A feral grin parted Karza's lips. "I can tell already. This is going to be fun."

General Akio had selected the building he was using as his command center in Tokyo partly because it was close to the Daisuke Corporation headquarters. Even so, the car ride took some time. The streets of the city were flooded with panicked civilians trying to escape the coming kaiju attack. The word about what was happening was out now, and despite the presence of General Akio's soldiers, Tokyo was in utter chaos. The general's limo was accompanied by two trucks full of armed troops, or even he and Karza might not have gotten through the various checkpoints his soldiers had set up. He was proud of the men under his command. They were truly doing the best they could under such grim circumstances.

The last reports he and Karza had received had brought both good news and bad. The only true kaiju to emerge from the ocean so far had been eliminated, and there was no sign of more of its kind. The winged kaiju who had engaged the American air wing and slaughtered it hadn't shown themselves above the city either. Both of those things were extremely good news. The bad news was that a literal army of lesser kaiju had come ashore in Tokyo's main harbor and were pouring into the city. His men were engaging the creatures throughout the city, but it was a hit-and-run type of game. His soldiers, as yet, hadn't been able to hold any position. They were being forced back as the lesser kaiju pressed forward. General Akio had more armored divisions in route to Tokyo, but by the time they reached the city, it was likely there wouldn't be anyone left to save. He wanted to turn loose the last of the helicopters and fighters at his disposal, but Karza had cautioned against it. If either the winged kaiju or more of the giant kaiju entered the city, they would be his only means of combating them, so he could see the wisdom in Karza's reluctance to deploy them at this point.

The front entrance of the Daisuke Corporation building was heavily guarded by mercs. Each of them armed to the teeth and not shy about breaking the bones or caving in the teeth of any panicked civilians who tried to gain access to the building. General Akio's expression was one of disgust as he watched one of the mercs bash the butt of the rifle he was carrying into the face of a teenager who refused to back up from the steps that led to the building's main door.

"Those guys are Black Company," Karza said. "They're the worst of the worst."

General Akio nodded. "I thought I recognized their uniforms."

"I'd wager Director Daisuke has at least two platoons worth of them in his employ. These jerks outside the building can't be the only ones."

Three of the mercs were approaching General Akio's limo. They were stopped by several of his soldiers. He knew from experience just how quickly such a situation could go south, so he opened his door and stepped onto the street.

In a booming voice that could be heard over the ruckus around the front of the building, he shouted, "I am General Akio. Director Daisuke is expecting me."

His bold declaration certainly captured the attention of the Black Company mercs. Their focus shifted instantly from his men to him. General Akio's soldiers stepped aside as he walked towards the leader of the mercs.

"Follow me, then," the leader of the mercs said. "But your troops remain here."

General Akio feigned a polite smile. "Thank you. That will be fine. However, my aide, Ms. Karza, *will* be accompanying me."

Karza had gotten out of the limo and stood behind General Akio. Her lithe figure only enhanced by the black business top she wore above its matching mini-skirt. The leggings she wore were black as well. Her hair was pulled up into a tight bun atop her head.

"You're American?" the leader of the mercs asked, his eyes moving over Karza's figure and lingering too long on the paleness of her skin.

Karza nodded. "Is that a problem?"

"No, ma'am," the merc replied in a thick Brooklyn accent.

General Akio grunted, signaling his impatience.

"Right this way, sir," he said with an edge of sarcasm.

The merc led them into the building's lobby where six more armed members of the Black Company stood guard.

"The elevator's right over there," the merc pointed. "I'll call up and let Director Daisuke know you're coming."

"Thank you," Karza told the merc.

When she and General Akio were inside the elevator and its doors had closed, she turned to him. "Those guys are going to be trouble."

"They already are," General Akio said, frowning. "I'd have them all arrested but…"

"Given the state of Tokyo at the moment, we don't need to turn this building into another war zone."

"Exactly," General Akio replied.

The doors of the elevator opened into the same wide, waiting room that General Akio had visited before. The receptionist was gone as was all pretense of welcome. Two Black Company mercs met them as they stepped out of the elevator and four more stood blocking the doorway to Director Daisuke's office.

One of the mercs who wore heavily tinted shades and a beret was clearly in charge of the others in the room. "Search them," he barked at the others.

Karza moved into the path of the two men who approached General Akio.

"This man is a general in the Japanese army," she informed them. "You will show him some respect."

All of the mercs broke into outright laughter. The two who had been approaching General Akio paused, staring at Karza. She met their stares without flinching.

"If you'll move aside, ma'am," one of them said to her. "We'll search you next. I promise."

"And we can make it take a while if you want," the other said, smirking.

General Akio saw Karza give him a questioning look. He sighed knowing what she was about to do if he gave the word. There was no one else in the room except for the two of them and the six mercs so he nodded.

The two mercs who had been ordered to search him began to move forward again, ignoring Karza. Neither of them saw her attack coming. She leaped into the air, the point of her right boot striking the closer of the two in the center of his neck. The man staggered backwards, clutching at his throat, his cheeks turning blue, unable to breathe. The other merc was too stunned to even move before Karza slipped by him and came up by his side. She slipped her arms around his neck and snapped it with a sharp cracking sound.

The leader merc with the shades yanked the barrel of the P-90 he was carrying up at Karza, but by the time he had, she was already on him. She yanked the weapon from his grasp with her left hand. The palm of her right hand slammed into his nose, over and over, as blood sprayed from his face with each impact.

General Akio's sidearm had cleared his holster by the time the other mercs began to come out of their shock and react. His pistol barked as he fired into the trio of mercs who remained outside Director Daisuke's office. Two of them were falling before the trio got off a single shot. One of the two mercs that General Akio had shot managed a wild burst from his weapon that ripped at the room's ceiling as he toppled over with a hole in his forehead. The third did return fire.

Throwing himself to the floor, General Akio avoided the burst from the merc's weapon that had been aimed at him, if barely. He heard the rounds whistle through the air above him. It was all up to Karza now. There was no way he could reposition him for another shot before the last merc swept his barrel downwards to end him.

General Akio heard a P-90 open up on full auto. Instinctually, he flinched at the noise, expecting the rounds to tear into him. When he realized he was okay and looked up, he saw Karza standing over him with the P-90 the merc with the shades had been holding, still smoking, in her hands.

"Get up, Akio," she told him. "We've got work to do."

Without waiting on him, Karza started for the door that led into Director Daisuke's office.

****

Nori stood in a corridor of Hell. *Well, at least that's what it looked like,* she thought. Somehow, Nori had managed to get Ruri through the city to the hospital they had set out for whatever good it was going to do. Ruri lay on a stretcher, barely conscious, and babbling about wanting her phone. It was still in Nori's pocket, and she had no intention of giving it back at the moment.

The entire corridor was full of injured people on stretchers. More rested propped against the walls of the corridor with relatives or friends kneeling beside them, trying to tend to them as best they could. The few nurses and members of the hospital's staff that Nori could see were clearly pushed past their limits. Their clothes and uniforms were smeared with red, and their bodies stunk of sweat. The wounded outnumbered them over a dozen to one. One nurse had given Ruri a quick look over before leaving her where she laid to move onto another patient. Nori had wanted to grab the nurse and demand that she help Ruri, but the patient the nurse had moved on to was a kid. The boy couldn't be older than six. There was no sign of his parents. He sat on the floor, shaking the stump that had once ended in his left hand. Drops of blood were flung from his stump onto the white of the corridor walls, spotting it with red, as he wailed loudly for his mother. The nurse was trying desperately to calm the boy without much luck. Nori couldn't so much as imagine the pain the kid had to be in. Finally, the nurse poked a needle into the side of the boy's neck. He slumped over, and as he had, the nurse started binding and applying pressure to his arm.

The soldier who had brought in the boy stood watching it all. He didn't look in too good of shape himself. Part of his face was badly burnt, and his eye on that side was swollen shut.

Nori had to look away from the nurse, boy, and soldier. She couldn't bear it all. Everywhere she looked, though, it was more of the same. Some of the wounded weren't screaming or even moving. She wondered if some of them had died waiting for help to get to them or had just been deemed too far gone by the overworked staff to waste time on, given how many others needed them.

Ruri grabbed her by the wrist. "Nori, take me home. This place is scary. I don't want to be here."

Nori felt tears welling up in her eyes as Ruri's grasp on her wrist went limp, and Ruri's fingers slipped off of her. Ruri had finally slipped fully into unconsciousness. Nori took Ruri by her shoulders and started to shake her but thought better of it. She wasn't a doctor and didn't know if that would be a good or bad thing to do. For all she knew, Ruri had a skull fracture and not just a concussion.

A male orderly in a red-stained medical smock appeared at the end of the corridor leading into the ER up ahead of where Nori stood beside Ruri waiting on help.

"The Kaiju!" the orderly shrieked. "They're in the building!"

The panic was instant. People began trying to get their loved ones to their feet and moving. Others grabbed the stretchers of the wounded lucky enough to have stretchers to rest on and started trying to roll them. The traffic jam and chaos in the corridor were hellish.

Nori wondered if she had fallen asleep, and this time, the Hell unfolding around her was really a nightmare as a kaiju came bounding around the bend of the corridor where the orderly stood and plowed into the man. It knocked him up against the wall and held him there with three clawed hands as its teeth gnawed into his throat.

The soldier who had brought in the boy with one hand jerked up his rifle, firing at the kaiju. The first burst from his weapon struck a fat woman who was trying to run. One bullet pierced her stomach, another her sternum, and the final one entered her body at the bottom of her throat. She collapsed to the floor as the panic in the corridor truly exploded. All traces of civilized behavior in the people around Nori were gone as they punched, kicked, and cursed each other, knocking over stretchers and spilling wounded loved ones onto the floor in the process.

The second burst from the soldier's rifle hit the kaiju. The bullets shredded the monster's side. Bulging purple snakes of its intestines poked through the wounds on its side, but the kaiju only seemed to grow angrier. It whirled to come charging through the crowd at the soldier as two more kaiju entered the corridor behind where Nori stood. The two monsters snarled as they worked their way through the panicked and trapped crowd, clawing and snapping at anyone unlucky enough to be near them.

Nori knew she had to do something fast. She couldn't just leave Ruri, though. She would never be able to live with herself if she did, no matter how annoying Ruri could be at times. They were friends, and friends didn't leave friends to be eaten by monsters.

Her head whipping about, Nori desperately looked for a means to get Ruri out of the corridor. She spotted a side door not far from where the two of them were. Nori grunted as she strained to lift her friend's unconscious form from the stretcher Ruri laid on. Ruri's body half-slid, half-fell from the stretcher into Nori's arms as she continued to struggle to support her weight.

Grunting and hurting with each step, Nori dragged Ruri towards the side door. Nori had no idea where it led or if she would even be able to open it. It was their only hope, though. The two kaiju working their way through the crowd behind them were getting closer, and the soldier ahead of them was dead now. The body of the kaiju he had shot lay on top of his corpse, half its head blown away from the final shot the soldier had been able to fire as its claws plunged into his heart.

As Nori reached the side door, a man came rushing up to it. He shoved her roughly aside, causing her to lose her hold on Ruri. Ruri thudded to the floor. It took everything Nori had just to stay on her feet, but she pulled it off, catching herself against the wall she had been shoved into. The man was yanking angrily on the side door. Apparently, it was either locked or barred somehow. His eyes grew wide as he let go of the side door and rocked in its frame. Someone or something was trying to get through it from the other side.

"You...!" Nori screamed at the man, but if he heard her, he showed no sign of it. The corridor was filled with the screams of the dying around them and the howls of the two lesser kaiju.

The door flew from its hinges slamming into the man. The impact crunched his nose as he was knocked from his feet. He landed hard on his butt, a dazed expression on his face, his nostrils leaking streams of red.

One of the lesser kaiju stood in the doorway. The kaiju's eyes glowed, a fierce, bright shade of yellow like a demon's might. It bowed its head as it came through to launch itself at the man. Its body was shaped like a man's but covered in matted, filthy fur that stunk of death and urine. The man screamed as he tried to roll away from the kaiju. It landed on top of him, tearing at him with the long, talon-like nails of its fingers.

Nori felt warm liquid running down her legs inside her pants and realized her bladder had released itself from the sharpness of her fear as the man's blood splattered over her. She couldn't reach Ruri where her friend lay on the floor without getting closer to the kaiju than she already was. Her body was heaving with sobs as she left Ruri where she lay and ran like hell. The man the kaiju had been attacking was dead. His body limp and most of his face, shoulders, and throat were little more than masses of mangled meat. The kaiju sprang from his corpse to chase after her as Nori pushed herself into the panicked crowd. She fought a path through those around like a demon, fists, nails, and elbows clearing her way and keeping those behind from grabbing her. The emotional pain of being forced to abandon Ruri filled her with a fury like she had never experienced before and gave her strength she didn't know she had.

She lost the kaiju as plowed into the crowd behind her. *There were plenty of people to keep it occupied,* she thought darkly, ashamed of herself. Nori spotted another side door and fought her way to it. It was locked too. She growled in anger, whirling about to catch a glimpse of the kaiju lifting an elderly woman's head into the air above the crowd as if showing off its latest prize.

A man with a fire axe took a swing at the kaiju. He buried the axe's head into the creature's side. The kaiju squealed in pain, bending over. The man jerked the axe's blade free and readied himself for another swing. The kaiju caught the axe by its handle as the man swung it. At the same time, its other hand shot forward, plunging into and through the man's guts. Blood bubbled onto the man's lips as the kaiju yanked purple strands of intestines from the man's abdomen, flinging them onto the corridor floor in curling piles. The man was long dead by the time the kaiju finally released his body to let it tumble over. Nori knew she had to keep moving. More of the kaiju had entered the crowd now, and the number of living people in the corridor was being thinned with each passing second.

Ahead of her, something *pinged*. Her heart leapt as she realized it was an elevator opening. She changed her course, hurrying past another kaiju that had a young woman pinned to the floor with its clawed hands and was snapping at her cheeks with its razor-like teeth. The kaiju was too preoccupied to notice her. She thanked God for that as she hurled herself into the elevator. There were two people in it. One was dead. Long, red slash marks stretched across his back, and he lay in a blood of still warm blood. The other was a woman, huddled in the elevator's corner, sobbing, with her head buried in her hands. Nori glanced into the corridor to see a new kaiju running towards the elevator. The thing had no eyes. Instead, it had a second mouth where its eyes should have been and sickening gray flesh that looked to be crawling with some kind of tiny eels or snakes. Its fingers rammed through the crack in the closing elevator doors, trying to hold them open. Nori dug into her pockets and produced the can of mace her father always demanded that she carry. She emptied it into the creature's upper mouth. The two-mouthed kaiju recoiled, gagging, and let go of the doors. The elevator lurched and began to descend.

"Where?" Nori snapped at the sobbing woman. "Where is this thing going?"

The woman didn't reply. She didn't even look at Nori. She just kept crying.

Nori ignored her. She needed a weapon. Dropping to her knees beside the dead orderly, she patted down his body and started digging through his pockets in the hope of finding something, anything she could use. A wallet, a cell, some chapstick, and a set of car keys were all the man had on him. As she finished her frantic search, the elevator pinged and its doors opened. Nori looked out to see that she had arrived at the hospital below the street-level parking area. The garage's lights were still on, and there was no sign of kaiju that she could see.

"You coming?" Nori asked the sobbing woman. Again, the lady didn't respond to her at all. Nori left the woman sitting in the elevator and darted out into the parking area. There were cars everywhere and not much else. Nori wished she knew how to hotwire one, but she didn't.

Following the directional signs on the walls of the parking area, she made her way to its exit. The smell of smoke washed over her before she was within a dozen yards of it. At first, she thought the hospital itself was on fire, but it wasn't. The smoke was coming from the wreckage of an overturned and burning ambulance outside. The flames danced wildly in the darkness of the night. The hospital had to be running on generator power because the rest of the city was black as midnight. It had been late afternoon when she had brought Ruri here. Had so much time really passed?

The thought of her friend caused her to stumble as she walked out of the parking area onto the street outside the hospital. She had left Ruri to die. Nori fell to her knees, looking up at the stars above, and prayed for forgiveness with tears streaming down her cheeks.

The distant sound of gunfire interrupted her prayers. *Where there was gunfire, there were soldiers,* Nori told herself. The gunfire was coming from somewhere south of where she was. Nori got to her feet, rubbing at the bruised and scraped skin of her bare knees. She was exhausted and her skin slicked with sweat and blood that wasn't her own. Still, if she wanted to live, she needed to get the soldiers. They could help her, keep her safe.

Without looking back at the hospital, Nori sprinted away into the night.

****

Director Daisuke was standing at the window behind his desk when Karza burst into his office with General Akio following closely on her heels. Karza had clearly been expecting more Black Company mercs to deal with, but there were none. Director Daisuke was alone.

"You could have just knocked," he said without turning to face them.

Karza started towards him wearing a feral snarl on her lips.

"Karza!" General Akio snapped.

Karza gave him a glare that chilled him to the bone, but she stopped where she stood.

"Director, you know why we're here," General Akio said.

Nodding as he turned, Director Daisuke moved to his desk.

"I do," he said calmly. "Your forces had failed to protect Tokyo from the kaiju and now, I suppose, it's to me to do so."

"That's one way to put it," Karza growled. "If you had been open with us and helped us from the beginning, this city might have stood a chance."

Director Daisuke shrugged. "The city is still standing, is it not? There is time left to stop the kaiju before all is lost."

"So then you do have a weapon capable of battling the kaiju?" General Akio demanded. "I thought you said you discontinued your father's work when you took over this corporation."

"I did," Director Daisuke smirked. "His work was obsolete. Archaic even, you might say, by today's standards. The future of Japan's defense does not rest in genetics and creating monsters to fight monsters. That only adds to the problem at hand."

"Get to the point," Karza spat.

"Project Kaiju, how can I say this? It *evolved* under my leadership of this corporation. We scraped my father's work and started fresh, this time with robotics and cybernetics."

"People are dying out there, Director," General Akio urged him. "We don't have time for this."

"Relax, General. Project Kaiju has already been activated. Even now, as we speak, it is powering up on the outskirts of Tokyo. My team there assures me that it will be ready to strike within the hour."

General Akio stared at Director Daisuke, urging the man to continue. What he really wanted to do was take hold of Daisuke and break every bone in the spoiled, rich bastard's body with his bare hands.

"That's fantastic." The sarcasm was thick in Karza's voice as she spoke. "But what in the devil is this Project Kaiju?"

"Why, Ms. Karza, it is the ultimate in Kaiju defense technology. And it's called Rei. Let me show you." Director Daisuke smiled widely, showing too-white teeth. He leaned over to push a button on the top of his desk. A twelve-foot panel slid aside on the side wall of the office to reveal an equally large screen. It came to life with the image of what looked to be a robot.

General Akio's breath caught as he realized the robot on the screen was gigantic. He could see the tiny shapes that must be engineers and techs moving about the workstations and mobile stairs that twisted about the robot's body. Rei, as Director Daisuke called it, was easily three hundred feet tall. The armor of its body was painted in bright reds and blues that sharply contrasted each other.

"That, my dear general and Ms. Karza, is Rei," Director Daisuke purred. "And I can assure you that he *will* bring to an end the kaiju rampage destroying this city."

"And this Rei is fully automated?" Karza asked.

"Yes," Director Daisuke replied. "Once Rei finishes powering up, he is programmed to destroy any and all kaiju he encounters. At that point, he will go dormant until a properly trained tech arrives safely deal with any damage he has taken and transport him back to his home facility."

"That's good to know." Karza grinned and threw herself at Director Daisuke. She moved across the distance between them in a blur, leaping over his desk to come crashing upon him.

"Karza! Stop!" General Akio yelled, but she wasn't listening.

"Wait!" Director Daisuke begged, "I am Tokyo's savior!"

That was all he got to say though before one of Karza's hands closed about his neck. The pointer and middle fingers of her other hand found his eyes and sunk into them. Director Daisuke wailed, struggling against Karza, as her fingers reduced his eyes to pulp in their sockets. Karza released him then, letting him drop to his knees in front of her. The blade of a knife flickered in the office's lightning as it came out from beneath one of Karza's sleeves.

"Don't do this!" General Akio raged.

The blade of Karza's knife slashed open Director Daisuke's throat in a single swipe. His blood exploded over her as she brought a foot up to his chest with near impossible speed to shove his dying body over the rest of the way to the floor.

"It's done," Karza said coldly as she turned to General Akio.

General Akio swallowed hard. "So it is," he said at last.

"You know he deserved it," Karza said, wiping the blade of her knife clean on one of the fancy curtains pulled back beside the office's window. "How many lives could we have saved if we had his toy when all this started?"

"Now isn't the time to discuss this." General Akio held up a hand in a gesture of peace. "Let's get back to the command center."

"Agreed," Karza nodded and then added, "My only regret is that the bastard didn't suffer more before he died."

General Akio led the two of them out of the office and through the corpse-filled waiting area to the elevator that would take them back to streets below.

****

Nori ran for her life through the streets of Tokyo. Bodies were everywhere. Wrecked cars blocked the roads. Buildings burned. They provided the only light in the other dark night. Storm clouds had rolled in cutting off the light of the stars and moon above. She could hear the hissing and grunts of the two kaiju behind her. One of them rushed after her, slithering on the ground, its body like that of a Black Racer. Yellow eyes blazed on the sides of the monster's diamond-shaped head. The heavy footfalls of the other crunched the pavement under its feet as it ran. The second kaiju's body appeared to be made completely of rocks cobbled together in the shape of a man. It shouldn't be able to move as fast as it did, but somehow, beyond all reason, it was.

The sound of gunfire called to Nori as she ran. With each aching movement of her legs and rasping breath, she drew closer to it. Her lungs felt as if they were on fire, and her heart thudded against her ribs inside her chest. If she could just reach the gunfire, she'd find help. The hope of doing so was all that kept her moving.

Nori rounded a corner and found herself staring into the barrels of several raised and ready assault rifles.

"Get down!" a soldier barked at her.

Nori threw herself to the pavement, skidding forward, carried by her momentum like a baseball player trying to reach home plate. She left a trail of smeared blood behind her as the palms of her hands and her bare kneecaps took the brunt of her impact.

The snake kaiju came slithering around the corner. The soldiers met with it a barrage of automatic fire. Bullets ripped and tore at the monster's flesh, biting deeply into it. This kaiju had no armor. Its scales really were like those of the snake it resembled. It reared up, stretching a towering nine feet into the air, as its body jerked about. Black blood burst from the holes the bullets made as they dug into it. With a final shrieking hiss, it slumped forward to thud onto the pavement and move no more.

Nori watched the soldiers take a step back from where she lay as the rock kaiju showed itself. Its hulking form rounded the corner. The monster had no mouth with which to roar, so it slammed its hands together in thunderous clap as it saw the soldiers. To their credit, none of them ran. They stood their ground and turned their fire onto the monster. Bullets pinged off its thick body, doing nothing more than chipping it where they struck. Nori could hear the CO of the group of soldiers calling for someone to fetch an RPG. Keeping herself as close to the ground as she could, Nori crawled towards the soldiers' ranks as bullets continued to whistle through the air above her.

The rock kaiju broke a large chunk of brick from the building next to it and hurled it into the soldiers. Two of them died as it crashed into them, breaking bones, and knocking them from their feet. The other soldiers kept firing. Their weapons were utterly ineffective against the monster, but the only other option available to them was retreat, and it was clear they were not going to do that.

Nori reached the soldiers. A dark-eyed young man took her hand, helping her to her feet.

"Get behind us," he ordered. "And stay there."

Nori wanted to hug the young man, but she did as she was told, hurrying out of his way. As soon as she was by him, he raised his rifle to his shoulder once more and took aim at the rock kaiju again. His rifle chattered, spent shells flying from its side to bounce at his feet.

A soldier came running up to where the current group was making its stand. In his hands, he carried a large weapon that Nori recognized as an RPG. She had watched enough to TV and movies know what it was. Nori hoped it would be enough to stop the rock kaiju.

Nori watched the man hastily take aim at the rock kaiju and fire the RPG he carried. It streaked from his weapon directly into the rock kaiju's chest where it exploded in a flash of heat and light. The rock kaiju blew apart from its center. Shards of the rocks that had once been its chest spun through away from its body. Two of the soldiers in front of Nori went down as the pieces of rock were flung from the blast to stab into them. A sliver of rock ripped into and through the first soldier's leg. He cried out as he desperately tried to yank the spear-like piece of rock shrapnel out of him. The other soldier who was hit died instantly. The rock that struck him smashed into his forehead just below the edge of his helmet, caving his skull inward. It hit with enough force that his eyes burst from their sockets in explosions of red.

"More kaiju approaching from the north!" one of the remaining soldiers shouted.

The burly soldier Nori knew must be the group's CO started waving a hand in the air. "Pack it up! We've got to fall back! Double time!"

Two soldiers Nori hadn't noticed before, who appeared to be working as a team, hefted a large gun that Nori thought was called a SAW from behind a pile of rubble. The bigger of the two men carried the weapon while the other looked to be carrying additional ammo for it.

"What about her?" the dark-eyed, young soldier asked the CO as he pointed in Nori's direction. "We can't just leave her!"

Nori stared at the group's CO as he appeared to be thinking over the young soldier's question.

"Sorry, lady," the CO told her after a moment. "Glad we could help you out here, but we have orders, and they don't include letting civilians tag along with us."

"I'm not leaving her," the young soldier told his CO.

"Private Ranmura, get your butt in gear. We need to move. Now!"

"No, sir. I'm staying here," Ranmura said again.

Nori looked at Ranmura and then at the CO. Both of them were on edge. The CO's finger rested lightly on the trigger of his weapon, and Nori could tell from how he stood that it would be easy for him to cut the private down where he stood.

"Fine," the CO snapped. "If we live through this, though…"

"I know what will happen, sir," Ranmura assured his CO.

The CO shifted his attention to the other soldiers. "What are you waiting for? Move the frag out!"

Nori stood with Private Ranmura watching the others bug out.

"Thank you," Nori told Ranmura. "I don't even know your name."

"You can call me Mura. Most folks do," he said, smiling at her.

"Why did you—?"

"Why did I stay?" Mura shrugged. "I had a sister. She was in the Navy. The monsters tearing this city apart killed her on their way here. She was aboard the flagship of the DESRON Samurai II when it was destroyed."

"I'm sorry," Nori whispered. "I lost my best friend to these things."

Even before she finished saying the words, Nori's emotions overpowered her, and she started sobbing.

"I think by this point, everyone in this city has lost someone," Mura told her, though he made no move to comfort her.

"Nothing we can do for them now except to try to stay alive ourselves."

Nori fought to get control of herself, wiping the tears from her eyes.

"Take this." Mura drew his sidearm and tossed it to her. "You know how to use it?"

Nori shook her head. Mura stepped closer to her, taking the pistol back. He showed her how to ready the weapon and how to work its safety. "Barrel at the kaiju, not me. Got it?"

Nori tried to smile as she answered. "I think I can handle that."

"The streets are teeming with kaiju," Mura said. "We can't stay out in the open like this too long, or we'll likely find ourselves in a fight we can't win."

"So where to?" Nori asked.

"I'm not from around here," Mura chuckled. "I was actually hoping you might know somewhere we could hole up."

Nori's forehead creased in thought. "It's a big city."

"Surely you have to know somewhere," Mura urged as he continued to keep his eyes and ears alert for signs of more kaiju closing in on their position.

Nori shrugged. "Not really. Not anywhere that would be safe from the kaiju."

"Okay then," Mura sighed. "I guess we go hunting. Try to keep up."

Mura took off, sprinting along the street. Nori ran after him, trying to match his pace.

With the power out in most of the city, the streets were dark other than the scattered fires of burning buildings and the flaming wreckage of crushed vehicles. They ran for a solid ten minutes before Mura skidded to a halt and held up his hand as a signal for her to do the same. His stop was so abrupt that she nearly collided with him, despite his warning.

The two of them stood on the corner of a street as Mura pointed to the road ahead of them. "That building there, it's as good as any we're going to find in this mess."

It was just like many of the other apartment buildings they had passed during their run. She wondered what made Mura pick it. Had he given up on finding anywhere safer?

"Why that one?" she asked.

"I don't know about you, but I am getting pretty tired of running. Besides, the longer we're exposed on the street, the more chance we have a kaiju or an entire pack of them spotting us."

Nori couldn't argue with Mura's reasoning. She was half-dead on her feet and she knew it. Her body couldn't take much more before it gave out on her.

"I'll lead. You cover me," Mura ordered and then started across the street.

They made it to the building's entrance without trouble. Nori didn't dare let herself hope that this area was clear of kaiju though as Mura tried the door. It nearly fell from its hinges when he touched it. Its frame was cracked and all, but one of the door's hinges was broken.

"Something forced its way in," Mura explained. He must have seen the concern in her eyes.

"Should we find somewhere else?" Nori whispered.

Mura shook his head. "Whatever did this couldn't be too strong or the door would be in pieces, not just messed up like this. Besides, it might not even be in the building anymore."

"I wouldn't count on that," Nori warned.

"I'm not." Mura grinned and shook his rifle at her as he said, "I am counting on this to handle it."

Together, they stepped into the darkness of the building's lobby.

"Hold up," Mura ordered, "And cover us."

The private shrugged his backpack from his shoulders, setting it on the lobby floor as he dug through its contents. He produced a pair of goggles. "Only got one pair of these so you stay close. Got that?"

"Yes, sir," Nori answered as Mura slid on the goggles.

She didn't need to be told that they were night vision goggles, and Mura must have known that because he took her by the hand and led them on without further explanation.

With the power off, the elevator was out. Nori was glad of that. She wasn't ever planning on setting foot on an elevator again for the rest of her life. Mura led them to a door that opened into a stairwell.

"Where do these stairs go?" Nori asked.

"They go up," Mura chuckled.

Nori stared at him as if he were an idiot.

"You don't watch a lot of American movies, do you?"

"Some," Nori shrugged.

Mura sighed. "Not the good ones then."

He took point as the two of them headed up the stairs.

****

General Akio and Karza had returned to the building they were using as their base of operations in Tokyo. The chaos in the city streets had died down a great deal on their return trip, just as a good portion of Tokyo's population had already died at the claws of the kaiju army invading it.

Wasting no time, General Akio had the staff of his war room locate Director Daisuke's massive robot, Rei. It had fully powered now and was moving into the city. It wasn't the only thing moving in the city, though. The kaiju leading the attack on

Tokyo had finally chosen to show themselves. There were two kaiju that stood over two hundred and fifty feet tall, respectively. One of them resembled something out the lore of the American author, H.P. Lovecraft. It was green, and the flesh of its body shifted about as if it was composed of nothing more than mist. Its mouth was covered by tentacles that writhed about wildly in the air. That was where the resemblance ended, though. Instead of having two legs, it had four. They were placed close together below its body, so close that each pair of them almost looked like a giant single leg. It also had four arms that were impossibly long. Each of them ended in a diamond-shaped, pointed head of a snake. The other kaiju was just as fearsome. It had no flesh to speak of. Its body was covered in a hardened exoskeleton. And two giant mandibles protruded from its face. Antenna waved about on the top of its head. The thing reminded General Akio of the American horror film *The Fly*, except this time, the film's protagonist had been merged with a giant ant and not a housefly. Both of these kaiju were walking ahead of the third and largest of the beasts, almost as if they were its personal guards.

The third kaiju stood close to four hundred feet tall. Great wings were unfolded behind its back, though it chose to walk and not fly into the city. Its head was covered in horns, and its eyes burned a bright blue. The scales covering its body were a slick color of black. The thing moved with an uncanny grace. General Akio knew instinctively that it was the leader of all the kaiju attacking the city.

"Daisuke's robot is on an intercept course for those kaiju," Karza informed him as General Akio took a seat in his chair at the center of the war room.

"Let's hope Daisuke's engineers knew what they were doing when they built it."

Karza flashed him a feral grin. "Looks like the show is about to start."

The robot, Rei, emerged from a street of buildings to step into the trio of kaiju's path. The great beasts paused as if they were unsure what to make of it. The tentacle-faced kaiju tilted its head as if intently studying the robot as Rei's arms came up. Missile launchers rose from the topsides of Rei's hands and then the battle began...

Three huge missiles flew from each of Rei's wrist launchers. All of them were aimed at the ant kaiju. Its head vanished from its shoulders in a flash of fire and heat. The kaiju's headless body stumbled backwards before it toppled over into a nearby building, shattering glass and bending structural support girders. As the kaiju's corpse slid to the street, the building came down on top of it.

The four-legged kaiju hurled itself forward at the robot, the snake heads that passed as its hands striking with lightning speed at Rei. Sparks flew each time on of the heads' fangs made contact with the robot's armor. They struck, over and over, so fast it was like watching a professional boxer go at a punching bag. Rei staggered under the blows but appeared unhurt. The robot caught one of the kaiju's arms as it lashed out towards it. Rei used both hands to snap the snake head arm. The white of bone protruded through the flows of mist-like green that covered the monster's true body beneath it. Rei paid for the pain it inflicted on the kaiju as one of the monster's other snake head hands collided with Rei's jaw, bending the robot's metal inward at the spot where it made contact. The kaiju pressed its sudden advantage, its other two snake heads whipping into Rei with enough force to bring the giant robot to its knees.

Rei looked up at the kaiju towering over it. The robot's eyes glowed yellow for a split second before beams of pure energy exploded from them. They raked over the kaiju's body from its waist to its throat, cutting the monster into two along its center. Green pus rained over Rei as the two halves of the kaiju fell apart. The globs of green pus stuck to Rei. General Akio could see smoke rising from them as if the pus were acidic and burning away at Rei's armor. The robot had no choice but to ignore the pus adhered to it as it got to its feet to face the leader of the kaiju.

The king of the kaiju already towered over Rei in height but its wings flapped, carrying it to rise just above the ground. It gave a roar that shook the entire city. General Akio felt the vibrations from the roar in his command chair. Windows of buildings blew out all over Tokyo, raining glass onto its streets.

Rei took a running start as it hurled itself at the king of the kaiju. General Akio watched in disbelief as giant-sized J.A.T.O. units popped out of the robot's back and ignited, adding speed to its charge. The robot slammed into the king of the kaiju like a running back. The force of Rei's momentum carried them both backwards towards docks of Tokyo's harbor and the ocean. The king of the kaiju told hold of Rei, the tips of its human-like fingers digging into and through the armor beneath them, to fling the robot away from it. The attack had injured the giant monster, though. Yellow blood seeped from the black scales that covered the king of the kaiju's chest. Its wings folded up behind its back as it landed in front of Rei.

Rei was damaged from the impact as well. One of the robot's arms dangled at its side, barely remaining attached to its body by strands of thick, sparking wires. Again, Rei opted to try its eye weapons as the king of the kaiju stroke calmly towards it.

The king of the kaiju's wings unfolded in a blur to swing forward, forming a sort of shield in front of it. Rei's eye beams flashed burning the wings, but to General Akio, it looked as if most of the energy of the beams were deflected away. As Rei's beam attack ended, the king of the kaiju parted its still-smoking wings and dove at Rei.

The robot made no attempt to dodge the great beast. Instead, Rei rose to meet the king of the kaiju as the monster came at him.

"Dear God in heaven, no," Karza rasped beside General Akio.

He knew what she was thinking. He was thinking it, too. The robot's computer brain must have analyzed the situation and deemed that it couldn't win the battle it was engaged in. It didn't take a hardened soldier like General Akio was to see that the robot was going for a suicide move. General Akio didn't have a clue what kind of power system Rei operated on, but he prayed it wasn't nuclear. A nuclear explosion on this level he feared would only finish what the kaiju had planned to do the city themselves not stop it. There was no time for General Akio or Karza to do anything but keep watching and see how things played out.

Rei didn't explode, but the robot's chest did open in its center. A blast of white-hot energy erupted from the opening in a beam that burnt a hole through the center of the king of the kaiju's body. The king of the kaiju howled in shock and pain, taking hold of Rei's head with its arms. They constricted about it with crushing strength. Rei's head, or rather what was left of it, snapped loose from atop the robot's shoulders. Sparks flew from the wreckage on the top of the robot's neck as its body collapsed at the king of the kaiju's feet.

General Akio held his breath as he watched the king of the kaiju closely. The wound Rei had dealt the monster appeared to be a lethal one but one never knew for sure when it came to kaiju. Rather than merely wait for the king of the kaiju to fall, General Akio took action.

"Scramble all our remaining fighters!" he yelled at Karza. "Let's make sure that monster goes down and stays down."

"Yes, sir!" Karza barked.

****

Something in Tokyo roared so loudly that both Nori and Mura dropped to their knees, hands clasped over their ears. The very stairs they had been climbing shook underneath them.

Mura was shaking his head as if to clear it as Nori removed her hands from her ears.

"What in the heck was that?" she asked.

"What?" Mura yelled at her. "My ears are still ringing! I can't hear anything."

Nori moved closer to him in the darkness of the stairwell, putting an arm around his shoulders to pull him to her.

"I said, what the heck was that?"

Mura heard her this time. "No idea," he said. "Couldn't be anything good, though."

Mura gently removed her arm from him. "We need to keep moving."

Nori nodded, knowing he could see her clearly through the night vision goggles he wore. Her eyes had adjusted to the darkness now, and she could at least make out the outline of things around her from the ambient light of the fires that came in through the windows at each platform between floors of the stairwell.

Mura started up the stairs but froze. A chill ran along the length of Nori's spine as he did so.

Sniffing at the air, Mura asked, "Do you smell that?"

"I can't really smell anything but smoke. Most of the city out there must be burning."

"There's something dead above us," Mura said, his voice going so soft and low that Nori could barely hear his words.

"How do you know?" she asked.

"I know what rotting meat smells like. My dad was a butcher," Mura whispered.

"Oh," was all Nori could think of to say in response.

"Hold on a sec," Mura told her. It looked like he was adjusting his goggles. Mura leaned out over the rail of the stairs and looked upwards. He jerked himself back onto the stairs in a quick motion, dropping to one knee as he vomited onto his boots.

That Nori did smell. Her own stomach turned at the scent, but she steeled herself and managed not to join Mura in his vomiting through sheer willpower.

When Mura stopped heaving, he wiped his lips with the backside of his hand.

"What is it?" Nori demanded. "What's up there?"

Mura apparently couldn't speak so he took off his night vision goggles and handed them to her.

Nori took them, sliding them onto her head by their strap, and leaned out of the stair's rail to take a look for herself. She wished she hadn't. From the floor above them, as far up as she could see, Nori saw the disemboweled and skinned bodies of men, and maybe women, it was hard to distinguish gender with so little left, hanging from the railing of the stairs by strands of their own intestines tied in cords around their necks. She did vomit then. Mura waited silently at her side until she was done.

"What...?" she started and had to pause to swallow, "What did that to them?"

"Kaiju," Mura said stating the obvious and only rational answer.

"If it was kaiju, where are they?" Nori asked, confused. Surely, if the monsters were in the building with them, they would have attacked by now.

"This place is a trap. We need to get out of here."

"No argument here," Nori said as Mura helped her to her feet.

A loud slamming noise echoed upwards from the bottom of the stairwell.

Nori flinched at the noise. "What was that...?"

"That was the main door to the stairwell on the ground floor," Mura replied. "I've tried all the others as we've been moving up the stairs. It's been the only one that was open so far."

"And now it isn't?" Nori's grip on the pistol Mura had given her grew tighter, her knuckles going white.

"Now it isn't," Mura confirmed. "They've locked us in here with them."

"We could still go up. Head for the roof or something," Nori suggested.

"That would be pointless," Mura explained. "Those things may be monsters, but they're not stupid. If they've blocked all the other doors in the stairwell, you can bet the top one will be blocked somehow too. There might even be more of the kaiju waiting for us up there."

"So what do we do?" Nori pleaded.

"The only thing we can, Nori," Mura said, his voice filled with half-hidden fear and sadness. "We fight or we die."

****

The snarls, growls, and hisses of the kaiju below their position on the stairs rose upwards from the ground floor. They were soon followed by the sound of inhuman feet charging up the stairs. Mura shot Nori a look.

"You have to keep it together if we're going to get through this," he cautioned her. "And don't shoot me in the back," he added as he ran to the corner of the platform they were on, angling the barrel of his rifle down at the stairs leading up to them.

Mura popped a flare and tossed it. It lit up the stairwell revealing the monstrous faces of the kaiju racing towards them. All the kaiju were humanoid. Each of them was covered in thick brown hair from head to toe and had the fanged snout of a boar that looked ready and eager to gore them. Some of the kaiju had lips smeared red with human blood.

Not waiting for them to get closer, Mura opened fire. His rifle chattered as it spat burst after burst into the ranks of the kaiju. The lead creature took several rounds in its chest and shoulders before it died. The others behind it trampled its body beneath them as they continued their charge. Mura kept firing. His next target took a burst to its head that splattered brain matter and bone fragments into the air. The kaiju died instantly. One of the kaiju behind it caught its corpse as the dead kaiju fell and flung it over the stair's railing out of its path. Mura's next target took multiple hits to its stomach that ripped into its innards, gutting it. Again, the kaiju behind simply flung it from their path.

"Anytime now!" Mura screamed at her as Nori stood gawking at the carnage he was creating in the kaiju's ranks. His words reminded her that she had a pistol in her hand. Not wanting to accidently shoot Mura, she leaned out over the railing and started firing at the approaching pack of kaiju from its side. Her first two shots missed. One of them sparked off the railing next to the kaiju. The other somehow streaked through the holes in their ranks to bury itself in the stairwell wall.

Nori steadied her aim and took a third shot at the monsters. This time, her bullet smacked into the skull of a pig-faced kaiju, destroying its left eye in the process. The dead monster careened sideways, colliding with another kaiju next to it. The two of them went down tripping up several of the others behind them.

"Yeah!" Mura shouted with excitement. "That's how you do it!"

In spite of their losses, the kaiju were gaining ground. They had closed to within yards of Mura's position. Mura flicked his rifle to full auto and hosed the front lines of their ranks. Kaiju howled and squealed. Mura held the trigger of his weapon tight until it clicked empty.

Nori saw him pop his expended magazine to reload. Mura had driven the kaiju back some with his desperate gambit but not far enough. The creatures plowed into him, knocking him over to pile on top of his prone body. Mura's pain-filled cries echoed in the stairwell. Nori fired into the kaiju that were swarming him, putting three rounds into the back one of them. The kaiju grunted and tumbled forward, disappearing into the pack. Nori realized there was nothing she could do to help Mura. His cries had already grown silent, and she didn't have the ammo to take on all the kaiju by herself.

Knowing she was next, Nori turned and darted up the stairs. The only weapon she had was the pistol Mura had given her, and there were far too many of the monsters left to try to make a stand with it. Her only hope rested in outrunning them. What she would do when she reached the top of the stairs and found the door there blocked, she had no idea.

Nori ran as fast as her exhausted and aching legs could carry her. She bounded up the stairs two at a time. Her breath came in ragged gasps. As she rounded the corner of the stairs, stumbling onto to the next floor platform, she saw the feet of the poor men and women who had been disemboweled and skinned dangling down from the railing above her. Nori forced herself to ignore the mutilated bodies and keep going. She could hear the footfalls of the kaiju behind her now. Those that hadn't stopped to feast on Mura were gaining on her fast. The toe of her right shoe hooked the edge of the next step, catching there. She lost her balance, unable to recover in time, and slammed into the steps in front of her. Nori felt a sharp pain in the side of her chest and knew she had cracked a rib or two in the fall. Her already-wounded kneecaps and hands were bleeding again. She left a trail of red drops in her wake as she heaved herself to her feet and pushed on. Nori knew she was that God had been looking after her, because the fall could have hurt a lot more than it had.

Glancing over her shoulder as she ran, Nori saw a dozen yellow, hungry eyes in the darkness of the stairwell looking up from below her. She didn't have a clue how many rounds were left in the magazine of the pistol Mura had given her. Fear and adrenaline had washed away her memories of not only how many shots she had already fired but also everything Mura had told her about the gun. Spotting a door that led onto one of the building's interior floors, Nori paused to try it. She jerked on its handle with all her strength. The door rocked in its frame but refused to open. She let go of the door and started running again.

The kaiju were so close now that she could smell them over the smoke and the stink of the bodies that dangled from the railing of each set of stairs she ascended. They had their own unique, musky odor. Nori knew that the top of the stairwell was only two floors above her. She had to think of something, do something to slow the kaiju.

As she rounded the last bend in the stairs and stepped onto the last floor platform of the stairs, she saw the doorway that led to the roof. A cool breeze blew in through it that gave her new energy as it touched her sweat-slicked skin. The door itself was gone. Only a pair of mangled and broken hinges rested on the side of the frame where the door would have been attached. Not taking any chances, Nori raised her pistol as she sprinted for the doorway and fired a shot through it into the night beyond. She hoped that if there was something waiting for her on the roof that the shot would drive it back from the doorway so that she could make it safely through.

The pain in the side of her chest was growing worse. She could taste blood in her mouth and wondered just how badly the fall on the stairs had hurt her. Her chest hurt with each breath she took. She prayed that her cracked ribs hadn't punctured one of her lungs. She didn't know anything about medical stuff. Before the kaiju had come to Tokyo, the worst injury she had ever had in her life was a broken knuckle from punching a bully in the nose…and that had been when she was eight.

Plunging through the doorway, Nori found herself in the cool air of the night outside. There was no sign for kaiju at least that she could see, but there was also no sign of the missing door that looked to have been torn off its hinges. The roof of the building was a wide, open space. Other than the small, shack-shaped protrusion of the doorway up from the building's interior, the roof was flat too. There was nowhere for her to hide. She had to make a choice of trying to hold the kaiju as they came through the doorway behind her or find a means to get off the roof before the kaiju caught up to her.

Nori whirled about, aiming her pistol at the doorway, though her eyes were still scanning around the rooftop. She saw what looked to be the top of a fire escape ladder not too far from where she stood. It became her back-up plan as she braced herself to take on the kaiju.

The first of the pig-faced monsters came through the doorway, grunting angrily at her. She squeezed the pistol's trigger and blew out the monster's right eye. The bullet exited the rear side of its skull in a spray of black blood that splattered over the other kaiju behind it. The next three kaiju all tried to push their way through the door's opening at once. They ended up in a tangled mess of arms and legs, each blocking the others. Nori used the time the kaiju had just bought her in their over eagerness to kill two more of them with well-aimed headshots. The third kaiju broke through as the bodies of the other two it had been wrestling against went limp. The third one was *fast*.

Nori had no time aim as it reared its head back in an inhuman roar and charged at her. Fear got the better of her in the moment, and she fired three shots into the monster in rapid succession. Her first shot slammed into the kaiju's chest with little effect in terms of slowing the monster, though it did blow a gaping hole in its ribs. Her second shot did much the same, striking the kaiju only inches from where the first shot had landed. Nori's third and last shot did the trick, though. She jerked the pistol a tad higher before she squeezed the trigger. That third bullet caught the kaiju in the center of its throat. Its roar turned into a sickening gargling noise as the thing choked on its own blood which flowed up into its mouth. Drops of black blood spattered across the floor of the roof as the kaiju shook its head about wildly trying to breathe. Nori retreated beyond the reach of its outstretched, grabbing arms as the monster stumbled towards her. She tried to shoot it again, but her pistol clicked empty. Not knowing what else to do, Nori threw the empty pistol at the monster's face and then turned to run towards the top of the fire escape ladder she had spotted earlier. Some still-functioning, rational part of her brain reminded her that she had seen six sets of kaiju eyes chasing her up the stairs. That meant there were three more of the monsters if that was truly all that was left after the battle she and Mura had fought on the stairs and she had counted correctly.

As Nori reached the top of the ladder, a kaiju that must have been hanging on the ladder just below the roof's edge, launched itself upwards at her. The thick mandibles protruding from its face snapped at her. She flung herself backwards, landing hard on her butt, as the kaiju pulled itself up and over the edge of the roof. The thing resembled a spider. It moved on six legs with two human-like arms on the sides of its body above them. The spider kaiju hissed as it climbed onto her body, pinning her beneath it. Nori punched and kicked at the monster, but her blows had no effect on it.

Nori screamed a final time as its mandibles snapped together on her neck, their ends meeting deep inside her flesh.

****

General Akio sat in his command chair as Karza stood beside him. The two of them watched together as several squadrons of fighters swept in on the wounded king of the kaiju. The great beast had dropped to one knee and looked on the verge of collapse. Rei's final blow appeared to have nearly finished it.

Waves of unrelenting missiles flashed as they hammered into the giant monster's body. Each explosion drew fresh blood from the king of the kaiju. Hurting as it had to be, though, the king of the kaiju still managed to put up a fight. A geyser of fire sprayed from its mouth to wash over two fighters as they came about for another run at it. The wings of the two planes grew misshapen as they melted in the heat of the flame before their own weapon payloads and fuel tanks erupted, causing the planes to become blossoming masses of fiery wreckage that blew apart in the sky.

The fighters were taking a heavy toll on the king of the kaiju, but General Akio could see that it just wasn't enough. He nodded at Karza. Karza moved to the nearby comm. station and opened a channel to the CO of the fighter squadrons engaging the monster.

General Akio couldn't fully hear the order she gave to the squadrons' leader, but he did catch the words, "Whatever it takes."

This time, as the fighters came howling, inbound towards the king of the kaiju, they loosed everything that had aboard them at the giant monster. Each plane emptied the entirety of its missile payload, all aimed at the king of the kaiju's head. Explosion after explosion tore at the monster. It reeled under the barrage unable to respond to it but still, it refused to fall.

Three of the fighters didn't pull up or veer away as they closed on the monster. One after the other, they drove themselves into the monster's skull. General Akio made a mental note to give each of those pilots the highest honors that he could as the king of the kaiju fell at last.

Entire sections of the king of the kaiju's massive head were caved in. The right side of its face had been stripped away down to the monster's very bones. A gaping wound that left brain tissue exposed to air leaked gray fluid on the top left corner of its fractured skull. One of its eyes was simply gone, leaving a burnt and mangled, empty socket in its place.

The staff of the command center around General Akio and Karza cheered and gave shouts of victory as the giant monster toppled over onto the streets of Tokyo and lay there unmoving as its own blood pooled about its body.

"It's over," General Akio said quietly.

Karza cocked her head in his direction. "No, sir, it isn't. We may have just won the war, but the battle is far from over. The entire city remains teeming with lesser kaiju."

General Akio gave a dark laugh. "Them we can handle Karza. See to it."

Karza nodded sharply. "Consider it done."

EPILOGUE

It took the better part of three days to clear the city of the lesser kaiju. Karza oversaw it all, every step of the way, and General Akio left her to it. He had his own problems to deal with. His plans to protect the city had failed and hundreds of thousands had died because of it. Worse, the attack had done so much damage that there was no hope of keeping it secret from the rest of the world as Japan had done in the past. The world now knew that kaiju were indeed very real, and that someday, more of the monsters would rise again to continue their war on the world of man. Press conferences, mounds of paperwork, and hearings lay ahead of him, and he could only hope that when they were done, he wouldn't have his rank stripped from him to be sentenced to the remainder of his life in jail. In truth, General Akio knew he had done all he or any man could do to hold back the monsters and that at least would allow him to sleep at night, regardless of where he rested his head.

THE END

Eric S Brown is the author of numerous book series including the Bigfoot War series, the Kaiju Apocalypse series (with Jason Cordova), the Crypto-Squad series (with Jason Brannon), the Homeworld series (With Tony Faville and Jason Cordova), the Jack Bunny Bam series, and the A Pack of Wolves series. Some of his stand alone books include War of the Worlds plus Blood Guts and Zombies, World War of the Dead, Last Stand in a Dead Land, Sasquatch Lake, Kaiju Armageddon, Megalodon, Megalodons, and Megalodon Apocalypse to name only a few. His short fiction has been published hundreds of times in the small press and beyond including markets like the Onward Drake and Black Tide Rising anthologies from Baen Books, the Grantville Gazette, the SNAFU Military horror anthology series, and Walmart World magazine. He has done the novelizations for such films as Boggy Creek: The Legend is True (Studio 3 Entertainment) and The Bloody Rage of Bigfoot (Great Lake films). The first book of his Bigfoot War series was adapted into a feature by Origin Releasing in 2014. Werewolf Massacre at Hell's Gate was the second his books to be adapted into film in 2015. In addition to his fiction, Eric also writes an award winning comic book news column entitled "Comics in a Flash." Eric lives in North Carolina with his wife and two children where he continues to write tales of the hungry dead, blazing guns, and the things that lurk in the woods.

CHECK OUT OTHER GREAT KAIJU NOVELS

KAIJU WINTER
by **Jake Bible**

The Yellowstone super volcano has begun to erupt, sending North America into chaos and the rest of the world into panic. People are dangerous and desperate to escape the oncoming mega-eruption, knowing it will plunge the continent, and the world, into a perpetual ashen winter. But no matter how ready humanity is, nothing can prepare them for what comes out of the ash: Kaiju!

RAIJU
by **K.H. Koehler**

His home destroyed by a rampaging kaiju, Kevin Takahashi and his father relocate to New York City where Kevin hopes the nightmare is over. Soon after his arrival in the Big Apple, a new kaiju emerges. Qilin is so powerful that even the U.S. Military may be unable to contain or destroy the monster. But Kevin is more than a ragged refugee from the now defunct city of San Francisco. He's also a Keeper who can summon ancient, demonic god-beasts to do battle for him, and his creature to call is Raiju, the oldest of the ancient Kami. Kevin has only a short time to save the city of New York. Because Raiju and Qilin are about to clash, and after the dust settles, there may be no home left for any of them!

CHECK OUT OTHER GREAT KAIJU NOVELS

MURDER WORLD | KAIJU DAWN
by Jason Cordova
& Eric S Brown

Captain Vincente Huerta and the crew of the Fancy have been hired to retrieve a valuable item from a downed research vessel at the edge of the enemy's space.
It was going to be an easy payday.
But what Captain Huerta and the men, women and alien under his command didn't know was that they were being sent to the most dangerous planet in the galaxy.
Something large, ancient and most assuredly evil resides on the planet of Gorgon IV. Something so terrifying that man could barely fathom it with his puny mind. Captain Huerta must use every trick in the book, and possibly write an entirely new one, if he wants to escape Murder World.

KAIJU ARMAGEDDON
by Eric S. Brown

The attacks began without warning. Civilian and Military vessels alike simply vanished upon the waves. Crypto-zoologist Jerry Bryson found himself swept up into the chaos as the world discovered that the legendary beasts known as Kaiju are very real. Armies of the great beasts arose from the oceans and burrowed their way free of the Earth to declare war upon mankind. Now Dr. Bryson may be the human race's last hope in stopping the Kaiju from bringing civilization to its knees.
This is not some far distant future. This is not some alien world. This is the Earth, here and now, as we know it today, faced with the greatest threat its ever known. The Kaiju Armageddon has begun.

SEVEREDPRESS

CHECK OUT OTHER GREAT KAIJU NOVELS

KAIJU SPAWN
by David Robbins & Eric S Brown

Wally didn't believe it was really the end of the world until he saw the Kaiju with his own eyes. The great beasts rose from the Earth's oceans, laying waste to civilization. Now Wally must fight his way across the Kaiju ravaged wasteland of modern day America in search of his daughter. He is the only hope she has left . . . and the clock is ticking.

From authors David Robbins (Endworld) and Eric S Brown (Kaiju Apocalypse), Kaiju Spawn is an action packed, horror tale of desperate determination and the battle to overcome impossible odds.

KUA MAU
by Mark Onspaugh

The Spider Islands. A mysterious ship has completed a treacherous journey to this hidden island chain. Their mission: to capture the legendary monster, Kua'Mau. Thinking they are successful, they sail back to the United States, where the terrifying creature will be displayed at a new luxury casino in Las Vegas. But the crew has made a horrible mistake - they did not trap Kua'Mau, they took her offspring. Now hot on their heels comes a living nightmare, a two hundred foot, one hundred ton tentacled horror, Kua'Mau, Kaiju Mother of Wrath, who will stop at nothing to safeguard her young. As she tears across California heading towards Vegas, she leaves a monumental body-count in her wake, and not even the U. S. military or private black ops can stop this city-crushing, havoc-wreaking monstrous mother of all Kaiju as she seeks her revenge.

CHECK OUT OTHER GREAT KAIJU NOVELS

ATOMIC REX
by Matthew Dennion

The war is over, humanity has lost, and the Kaiju rule the earth.

Three years have passed since the US government attempted to use giant mechs to fight off an incursion of kaiju. The eight most powerful kaiju have carved up North America into their respective territories and their mutant offspring also roam the continent. The remnants of humanity are gathered in a remote settlement with Steel Samurai, the last of the remaining mechs, as their only protection. The mech is piloted by Captain Chris Myers who realizes that humanity will not survive if they stay at the settlement. In order to preserve the human race, he leaves the settlement unprotected as he engages on a desperate plan to draw the eight kaiju into each other's territories. His hope is that the kaiju will destroy each other. Chris will encounter horrors including the amorphous Amebos, Tortiraus the Giant turtle , and the nuclear powered mutant dinosaur Atomic Rex!

KAIJU DEADFALL
by JE Gurley

Death from space. The first meteor landed in the Pacific Ocean near San Francisco, causing an earthquake and a tsunami. The second wiped out a small Indiana city. The third struck the deserts of Nevada. When gigantic monsters- Ishom, Girra, and Nusku- emerge from the impact craters, the world faces a threat unlike any it had ever known - Kaiju . NASA catastrophist Gate Rutherford and Special Ops Captain Aiden Walker must find a way to stop the creatures before they destroy every major city in America..

 SEVERED**PRESS**

CHECK OUT OTHER GREAT KAIJU NOVELS

MURDER WORLD I KAIJU DAWN
by Jason Cordova
& Eric S Brown

Captain Vincente Huerta and the crew of the Fancy have been hired to retrieve a valuable item from a downed research vessel at the edge of the enemy's space.
It was going to be an easy payday.
But what Captain Huerta and the men, women and alien under his command didn't know was that they were being sent to the most dangerous planet in the galaxy.
Something large, ancient and most assuredly evil resides on the planet of Gorgon IV. Something so terrifying that man could barely fathom it with his puny mind. Captain Huerta must use every trick in the book, and possibly write an entirely new one, if he wants to escape Murder World.

KAIJU ARMAGEDDON
by Eric S. Brown

The attacks began without warning. Civilian and Military vessels alike simply vanished upon the waves. Crypto-zoologist Jerry Bryson found himself swept up into the chaos as the world discovered that the legendary beasts known as Kaiju are very real. Armies of the great beasts arose from the oceans and burrowed their way free of the Earth to declare war upon mankind. Now Dr. Bryson may be the human race's last hope in stopping the Kaiju from bringing civilization to its knees.
This is not some far distant future. This is not some alien world. This is the Earth, here and now, as we know it today, faced with the greatest threat its ever known. The Kaiju Armageddon has begun.

CHECK OUT OTHER GREAT KAIJU NOVELS

KAIJU WINTER
by Jake Bible

The Yellowstone super volcano has begun to erupt, sending North America into chaos and the rest of the world into panic. People are dangerous and desperate to escape the oncoming mega-eruption, knowing it will plunge the continent, and the world, into a perpetual ashen winter. But no matter how ready humanity is, nothing can prepare them for what comes out of the ash: Kaiju!

RAIJU
by K.H. Koehler

His home destroyed by a rampaging kaiju, Kevin Takahashi and his father relocate to New York City where Kevin hopes the nightmare is over. Soon after his arrival in the Big Apple, a new kaiju emerges. Qilin is so powerful that even the U.S. Military may be unable to contain or destroy the monster. But Kevin is more than a ragged refugee from the now defunct city of San Francisco. He's also a Keeper who can summon ancient, demonic god-beasts to do battle for him, and his creature to call is Raiju, the oldest of the ancient Kami. Kevin has only a short time to save the city of New York. Because Raiju and Qilin are about to clash, and after the dust settles, there may be no home left for any of them!